This edition first published 2017 by Fahrenheit Press

10 9 8 7 6 5 4 3 2 1

www.Fahrenheit-Press.com

F 4 E

Speed Of Life

By

James Pate

Fahrenheit Press

For Carrie,

Prologue

Outside Johnson, Mississippi. 1973.

In the back of the van were two men, both naked except for their underwear and the burlap bags over their heads and the handcuffs on their wrists. Liz drove the van south through a night so black and dense only the stretch of space in front of the headlights was visible.

Horace smoked calmly on the passenger side and told her about his brother who was a cop in Chicago. As he spoke, she realized how little she knew about him, even though they had been friends, or at least business acquaintances, since the late sixties. "I make more than him and it drives him up the fucking wall," Horace was saying about his brother. He had a high voice that seemed to come from a spot behind his eyes. "I send Mom about one-fifty a month. That's more than he can ever give her. He tells her not to take it, tells her I'm a nasty son of a bitch who makes his money by unlawful means, but she does. She takes it. I always was her favorite. Her angel. It's because I'm so small, because I look so delicate. People assume they have to protect me. God gave me a great gift, making me this size."

"Where does she think the money comes from?" Liz asked.

"When I write, I tell her I work as a mailman, and mailmen get paid a lot better than people think. She believes me because it's me saying it. My brother tells her I'm lying, but she thinks he's just jealous, me being a mailman and all, and him being just a cop." He brought the cigarette to his mouth.

They turned down a gravel road. The headlights shined against the branches hanging low over the lane. Her own mother had been a whore in Little Rock and she had a little room with a bed off of the den where she took the men. Liz would be upstairs in the small house, reading by the window or trying to sleep. She would hear her mother and she would hear the men. At school the other kids knew and one boy carved MY UNCLE FUCKS YOUR MAMA on the wood of her desk with his compass. Liz told Horace, "What do you think is worse, having a whore for a mom or a cop for a brother?"

"Shit. I don't know, Liz. Hard choice."

"I'd pick the cop as a brother over the whore for a mother. Nothing wrong with a cop, long as he isn't out for blood or corrupt or some shit like that." The van rolled over a cluster of twigs, snapping them.

"Most of them are. Out for blood or corrupt, I mean."

"Yeah, I guess so. Your brother like that?"

"Between the two of us, I'm the nice one, if you can believe that."

"You're right. I can't."

Liz turned the van on to an even more narrow gravel lane. They drove for half a mile, deeper into the trees and shrubs. The darkness was total. The headlights, turned up to their highest beam, illuminated the road and flanking shrubs but everything outside of the light was black.

She said to Horace, "You ever wish you were a cop like your brother? Be a lot less stressful."

"No way," he answered. "A guy my size? Every cop I knew in Chicago, they weighed over two hundred pounds and had arms the size of lambs. I would've looked like a munchkin beside those guys. You look at me with them and you'd think I was about to sing about the yellow brick road."

"You are on the small side."

"Take a guess."

"What do you mean?"

"About my size. Take a guess."

"Five six."

"Off by two inches."

"Two inches going up?"

"Shit, you're only trying to flatter me now. Going down."

"You never look it."

"Don't you ever wonder why I wear these big ass boots, with these big ass heels?"

They went over a bump. The jolt caused the radio dial to shift and static came in through the speakers. Neither of them bothered to switch it back to the station.

Liz glanced over at him. "Your turn to guess."

"How tall you are?"

"No. How much I weigh. People look at you and they see how short you are and people look at me and see how fat I am. So guess."

"I am not about to tell a lady what I think she weighs. What kind of fool do you have me pegged for?"

"Over three hundred or below?"

"Shit. I told you I'm not saying."

She laughed and told him to light her a cigarette.

They parked the van under a dogwood tree. It was early spring. White petals were on the dogwood branches and the air was heavy with the scent of things in bloom. She and Horace climbed out of the van, walked to the back doors. Horace was in his black T-shirt and Liz had on her black leather jacket and gray cap, an outfit inspired by the one Brando wore in The Wild One. From her jacket pocket she took out a pair of white leather driving gloves. She carefully tugged them on. She flexed her fingers inside the gloves.

She opened the back door of the van and started pulling on the chain attached to the two handcuffs. She told them, "You two taking a nap?"

They nodded no. Under the burlap bags their mouths were covered in masking tape. They rose blindly and with their hands felt around the van and she took them by the wrists and helped them step out. One guy was deeply tan and the other had skin so white it looked like it would bruise if you

3

ran a finger along it. She walked ahead and led them with the chain as if they were dogs, except the chain was fastened to the cuffs around their wrists and not around their necks. Horace was behind the three of them, whistling. Twigs broke under their steps. Liz held a flashlight in one hand, the chain in the other.

She said, "The place we have to get to, it's not that far."

They came to a field. The grass was damp from recent rains. The whole area belonged to a friend of Horace's, a guy named Jimmy that Liz had only met a handful of times. He was skinny and leathery-skinned, with long gray hair he wore in a ponytail. He rarely spoke. And when he did talk he liked to tell people about how the mafia killed JFK and Black Panthers had killed Martin Luther King and how the moon landing was Hollywood hocus pocus and that the closest anyone had ever gotten into outer space was a few miles above the earth and nothing more. Liz wasn't sure how Horace met Jimmy. She asked him once and he'd said God had a way of bringing people together. Jimmy lived in a white farmhouse nearby and he owned several acres around the farmhouse. Liz was sure Jimmy was paid for allowing her and Horace to use his grounds on nights such as this.

Her sneakers were getting wet as they trudged through the thick grass.

After another five minutes of walking they approached a small pond. She stopped walking, and told the men, "We're not going to kill you. You two assholes don't have to worry about that. You're going be punished but you're not going be killed."

Horace stabbed his cigarette into his mouth, took off the burlap bags. The two men, once free of the hoods, breathed heavily and their eyes were damp and wide. Liz said, "If I remove the tape form your mouths, you going be quiet?"

Both nodded.

She stepped toward them and yanked the tape from one of them and then the next and tossed both pieces on the ground.

4

One of the men, the tanned one, said, "I'll do whatever you say. You guys won. I won't ever try that shit again."

"You made that promise before, if I remember correctly," Horace said.

"I ain't joking," he said.

The pale one sobbed, kept wiping his cheeks with the backs of his cuffed hands.

"Even if I believed you," Horace explained, "you still need to get punished. So think of what's about to happen to you not as something to keep you from selling in that area in the future, but for selling in that area in the past. Maybe thinking about it that way will make it easier."

He flicked his cigarette at the tan one's face.

Liz said, "Look here, you two." She threw the beam of the flashlight under a pine tree about ten yards away. The beam revealed two long pieces of woods with rope hanging from the edge of one of them. Then she lowered the beam and it showed a huge hammer and a few long nails. The pale one started sobbing loudly. The tan one tried to run but Liz expected this and held on to the chain and he pulled and pulled and she laughed and held on. Horace jogged up and kicked at the man's legs and after the man fell Horace kicked repeatedly at his back. The tan man whimpered please, please, please.

The pale guy lowered his hands from his face, his body trembling. He said, "I'm going to remember this. The only way I'm not is if you kill me."

Liz shook her head. "You aren't important enough to be killed."

"Fuck you."

Liz walked up to him, struck him hard in the face, the stomach. He crumpled up, bending at the waist and knees. He fell to his side. She stood back and eyed him, seeing if he would move. The breeze shook the leaves over her head. She heard them. In the quiet of the night they sounded like thousands of wings beating and fluttering and on the verge of launching off into the night sky.

His body remained inert.

She looked up at Horace. "You mind making us some coffee? I imagine this won't be a short night for any of us."

He nodded yes. He trudged up the nearby hill and toward the house with the lighted downstairs windows in the distance. She watched until she could no longer see him through the trees and shrubs. She sighed and reached down to pick up the hammer. The one she'd struck lifted his head. He sat up with his hands cupped behind his neck. He stared at the grass near his feet and said, "It ain't fair and you and your asshole friend know it. Max and me, we've been dealing in that neighborhood for years now. And your friend comes in, bosses us around, and starts taking over. He don't have no right. That area was ours."

"Yeah. It was yours. Horace and his people, it's their turf now."

"I don't mean no offense, miss, really I don't, but what gives him the motherfucking right?"

"I give him the right. That's all you need to know."

She picked up a long plank of wood from under the tree and brought it over to the two men. She threw the plank down. It made a nice hard sound against the earth. She turned to the one she had been speaking with and said, "You drove the nails in yourself. You remember that as I do this, you hear?"

He glared at her, his eyes brimming with wild, speechless hate.

"Think of it this way," she said. "Not many people go through what you're about to go through. If you live through this you'll have something to brag about."

Next to the pine set a leather bag the size of a shaving kit and she unzipped it and took out two needles. Neither of the two men protested as she injected the heroin into their arms. Soon she had them arranged: their arms tied to the planks of wood, the burlap back over their heads. She glanced at the house and wondered what was taking Horace so long with the coffee. Then she picked up the hammer.

At the age of thirteen she had been reading Robinson Crusoe in the chair by her window when she saw a blue truck speed up to the house and stop. Her mother was in the bed of the truck, naked and with her arms tied behind her back and her head shaved. Three men came out of the cab of the truck and one had no shirt and another wore ragged overalls and her mother's fancy violet hat and the other wore all black and they dragged her from the truck and threw her into the yard. She cursed at them, called them names. Two of the guys held her down as the one with her hat on his head crouched over her and spat on her face and wiped his mouth with the back of his hairy wrist. Then the three were back in the truck and the truck was gone. Her mother was there, in the thick grass. She was there, breathing hard. Liz watched wanting to go down into the yard and yet not doing so. The feeling was more than fear. It was more than anything she had ever thought or felt or had conceived of. Some minutes later her mother rose and walked into the house. Liz remained in the window, her eyes on the empty yard.

"You will want to scream," she said to the man as she placed the nail in his sweaty palm, "but try really hard not to. I don't reckon anyone will hear you but you don't want to take that chance anyway, okay?"

He nodded. She'd fixed the flashlight into the groin of a tree, aiming the beam so she would have a light to work by. She gave him a warning before she brought the hammer down. She told him it was coming. And it came.

Part One: After the Funeral

April 1978

One

By late morning it was not so bad in the KC's Cafe on Summer Avenue. The breakfast crowd had left. Oscar wasn't frantically scrambling eggs and bacon and trying to keep the various orders in his head.

He had time to take off his apron and pour a cup of coffee and leave the kitchen. When he stepped out from the back he saw the place was almost empty. Oscar stood at the jukebox, smoking a cigarette and flipping through the jukebox menu. The kitchen phone rang. He heard Ruby pick it up. She was a waitress in her fifties who always looked like she'd had two hours of sleep the night before. She stood out from the kitchen doorway, telling him he had a call.

"You sure it's for me?" he asked.

"They asked for you by name, honey."

He took the phone from her and walked into the pantry, where there was more privacy. He heard Brian say, "Hey man, got some real fucked-up news to share." Brian was a local piano player, songwriter and producer. Oscar had known him since the late sixties, and in the mid-seventies they'd made a record together, Brian doing production and Oscar doing almost everything else. He said, "Tommy's dead. They found him in a hotel room in Tucson. Looks like it was an overdose. A heroin overdose."

Oscar leaned his elbow against the lime-green wall of the pantry and scratched the back of his head. Tommy had been in a band with him called Cosmic Dust back in the first few years of the decade. He'd moved to Tucson only two months ago. "Well, shit," Oscar said. "That is some fucked-up news."

"I know you two were at odds sometimes but I also know you guys were close at one point too. That's why I'm calling you first. I just heard myself five minutes ago."

"Yeah, thanks. I'm glad you did. How did you hear about it?"

"His dad knows my dad, that's how I heard. His dad knew me and him were friends, so he called my dad, and my dad told me."

"Shit. When's the funeral?"

"I don't think that has been settled yet. I'll let you know, man."

"I hate to hear it but I'm not surprised."

"About his death?"

"Yeah, from an overdose. These past few years, I can't think of a time when I haven't seen him fucked-up. You know how he was."

"We all do some hard living."

"He was going at it hardest."

Oscar saw two customers walk into the diner and take the booth near the jukebox, two men in denim jackets. He said, "I should get back to work. The manager doesn't like us using the phone too long."

"Okay. You go fry those burgers now," Brian said.

"Anything you need me to do? Anybody you want me to call?"

"If anybody comes to mind. I guess I'll be on the phone the rest of the day, spreading the word."

Shortly after the call the lunch crowd began coming in. Oscar fried patty melts. He ducked wire baskets of frozen potato slices into simmering vats of oil. As he worked and as the jukebox played a string of Donna Summers songs he thought about Tommy. He imagined Tommy dead in a sweltering apartment in Arizona, flies hovering around his lifeless face and open eyes, curtains closed and keeping out the blazing sun. Cosmic Dust had broken up four years before, in the summer of seventy-four, and Tommy had left the band a year before that, but the two of them had kept in touch. And when Oscar had moved to Manhattan for a year in the mid-seventies Tommy had crashed at his place several times. But in the past year they'd drifted apart. Tommy drifted away from most of his old friends. He started looking very sick and frail and his bushy black hair started hiding his face. He looked like he weighed ninety pounds.

His old friends knew what was going on. His old friends knew he was sinking. And now he'd sunk, not quite making it to his twenty-ninth birthday.

Two

The funeral was at a Baptist church on the corner of Summer Avenue and Highland, a dark-brick building with a white steeple. The service was packed with Tommy's high school friends and music friends and his large family. His mother and his father had been divorced for years and they sat in different pews and did not speak to one another before the service. Oscar chose a seat in the back with his cousin Juanita. The minister was a bald man with thick glasses who walked with a limp. From outside you could hear traffic streaming by and kids shouting to one another as they rode down the sidewalk on bikes.

After the funeral Oscar and Juanita smoked cigarettes in front of the church, watching the mourners in their cars follow the hearse to the cemetery out east, near Germantown.

"You positive you don't want to go too?" she asked.

Oscar shook his head.

"It's a little amazing how the minister never once brought up drugs. Just talked about a confused and sad generation."

"He probably never met Tommy." He shrugged. "Tommy would've liked it though, I bet. The minister was trying to make him into some tragic figure and that's certainly how Tommy saw himself."

"He did bring up the music."

"Yeah, the gift of song. He never got very specific."

"He probably never heard of Cosmic Dust."

"That would make him like pretty much everyone else."

Oscar dropped Juanita off at her house in Midtown since she had to work at Pop Tunes that evening. Then he met Brian and a few of their friends at the Friday's on the corner of Overton Square. There were four of them in the booth by the dusty window: Oscar and Brian and Brian's wife Janice and Janice's sister Helen, who had briefly dated Tommy. Oscar nibbled on his cheeseburger and drank from one shot of whiskey after the next. Brian had already gone through four beers and was red-faced. He was saying, "Tommy had this haunted quality, you know, as if he was already half a ghost."

Janice added, "He was like a child. He would get hurt so easily. He wasn't really right for this world. I know that's a sentimental thing to say, but I really do believe it." She wore a black dress with a lacy white collar. She looked numb, as if she'd been on Valium the entire day.

Oscar took a sip from his whiskey. "I haven't seen him since November and the last time I did he called me an asshole."

Everyone at the table glanced up at him. Janice kept her eyes on his face as she brought a cigarette to her lips. He added, "I think he hated me by the end. I hope that's not true but I suspect it is."

"That's not true at all," Brian said. "He had complicated feelings about you."

"He had complicated feelings about everything," Helen said.

"Why did he call you an asshole?" Brian said. "Knowing you, I suspect he had some good reasons for it."

"Screw you," Oscar said. He glanced up at Brian and grinned.

"Come on. Don't pretend to get all sensitive."

Oscar said, "This was in New York about a week before Thanksgiving. We had this mutual friend and we were staying at his place on the Upper West Side. We were up there to see some shows, just fuck around, no big deal. This

---

13

one night, we got drunk at this club and started walking around in the rain and for some reason he started going on and on about this guitar he'd lent me when we first met. He was making the claim when I returned the guitar to him a few days later, it never sounded right. He worked with it and worked with it but never could get the sound right again. Then he said that was me all over, everything I touched turned to shit, everything I touched fell out of tune. So I told him his guitar was probably fucked to begin with and he probably lent it to me knowing he would then be able to blame the guitar's fucked-upness on me if he did. That was when he gave me this look and called me an asshole. After that I went back to the friend's apartment and Tommy went to the bus station and waited around until he could catch one going back to Memphis."

"He didn't even go back to get his stuff?" asked Janice.

"He liked to carry his shit with him," Oscar said. "He tended to travel light anyway."

Helen asked, "That was the last time you saw him? That was five months ago. I always figured you two were closer."

"I'd talk to him on the phone. I never saw him again, though."

By midnight Oscar and Brian were the only ones from the funeral still at Friday's. Oscar said, "Brian, there's this thing I've been thinking about. I've been thinking about it ever since you called me at KC's with the news."

"About Tommy?"

"Yeah. About Tommy."

"What is it, man?"

"Back in March I got this phone call from him. It must've been about three in the morning. He told me he'd moved to Tucson, which I already knew, but then he said something I've been thinking about these past few days. He said he'd gotten in trouble in Memphis, and that was why he left. I thought he meant legal shit, you know? Something to do with the police, like maybe they caught him with heroin. I asked him about it, but he just said it was trouble, pure and simple. Trouble was trouble and it didn't really matter where it was coming from. That's what he told me. Which is such a bullshit Tommy kind of answer, right?"

"Sounds just like him."

"Then he said if anything should happen to him, it wouldn't be an accident. He said it in this serious voice. It was so serious I thought he was kidding me at first."

"Shit, Oscar. That is weird."

"He said if he was run over and killed by a car it wouldn't be an accident. He said if a safe or a piano happened to fall on his head while he was walking around Tucson, that wouldn't be an accident either. He said, 'Oscar, I've reached a point in my life where there are no accidents.' I asked him what the hell he meant. It was the middle of the night and I'd been asleep when he called and I was pissed. I hadn't heard from him in months and here he was, telling me this cryptic bullshit. But he just said to remember what he told me, and he hung up."

A paper airplane zipped through the air over their heads and swirled down and landed in Brian's mug of beer. Brian lifted it from the mug, pinching it out with his thumb and index finger. A man in corduroy shorts and white tennis shirt came over, apologizing, saying, "I'm sorry, man. I didn't think it would fly all the way over here. You want me to buy you another beer?"

"I've been here since three o'clock," Brian said. "I reckon I've had enough." He handed the plane back to the man and the man bowed and left the table and walked across the room to a booth filled with young women whose faces and arms were burnt from the sun.

Oscar and Brian were parked in the lot behind Overton Square. Brian was a big man, about six-three or six-four, and fleshy, just shy of being fat. He walked slowly. His eyes were on the sidewalk. Oscar noticed that he had on sandals, sandals he must've worn to the funeral. "To tell you the God's honest truth, I don't know if Tommy's call meant much," Brian said. "He was prone to wild flights of fancy.

One day he'd talk like a saint from the twelfth whatever century and the next you'd think he was William Burroughs Junior, going on about the sanctity of drugs. It would not surprise me in the least if he knew his time was coming because of how much shit he was putting into his body and it also wouldn't surprise me if he wanted to fuck with your head a little by giving you that call. For a dude that never smiled, he could have a sense of humor."

"You might be right about that. You know, I didn't really know him all that well. People think I did but I didn't."

"You two made some beautiful music together."

"You don't need to know someone that well to do that. Music isn't as personal as people like to think it is. It's out there." He gestured to the night around them. "It's not in here." And he pointed to his temple.

"Maybe for you," Brian told him, taking his keys from his pocket. "Think it was different for Tommy. I doubt that dude ever wrote a thing he didn't think was composed with his own blood."

Three

His uncle lived in a one-story fieldstone house on South Parkway across the street from Overton Park. His name was Franklin Evans and he was an art photographer.

A few nights after Tommy's funeral, Oscar went over to Frank's place. Juanita had called him, telling him her father would be showing a Warhol movie, and that he should come over because it would help take his mind off Tommy. Frank was constantly flying back and forth between New York and Memphis. When he was in New York he stayed with his girlfriend in the Chelsea Hotel, a woman named Violet. And Violet had been close to Warhol and his group, close enough that she appeared in several of his films. Frank would sometimes borrow one of the film reels from her. He would screen them in his house in Memphis on a sheet he nailed to the wall of his living room.

Frank answered the door. He wore houndstooth check pants and a white dress shirt. He was a handsome dark-complexioned man in his mid-forties. "Come in, come in," he said with his heavy Mississippi drawl. From that drawl you could tell he wasn't from Memphis. In Memphis, people tended to speak faster, with a curl at the end of the sentences, as if asking you a question the speak speaker already knew the answer to. "You arrived just in time."

Oscar took his sneakers off in the vestibule. He placed them next to the other shoes lining the wall. "Heard you're showing a movie."

"Yes, indeed. Violet is here. She brought one of her films. I started the projector right before I heard you knock."

"One of the Warhol ones?"

"It's called Naked Cowboy Diner. It's about naked cowboys in a diner. Violet is in it. She is the one non-cowboy character."

Oscar followed Frank into the spacious high-ceilinged living room. It was dark and several shapes were sitting around on the sofa and the floor. Oscar could make out the faces in the light of the film playing on the sheet. Violet was there, in a black crochet dress, her arms stretched out along the back of the couch. Juanita was there, sitting on a hassock with a cocktail in her hand, her straight hair hanging down to her waist. And Freddie was present too, a balding junkie in his fifties Frank liked to hang out with. He appeared in one of Frank's photographs naked to the waist and holding an antique gun across his skinny chest.

Oscar took a seat on the floor. Frank lurked in the back of the room, standing by the film projector and smoking and looking like a thin apparition who might disperse into smoke too and fade into the ceiling.

The film was either silent or the sound wasn't working. Bach organ music played from Frank's expensive stereo system in the den next to the living room. Violet roamed around a diner wearing nothing but an apron. A few muscular clean-faced men in cowboy hats were at the tables, all of them eating steak. They were nude too with the exception of their cowboy hats and the bandannas tied around their necks. The diner seemed dirty. It was easy to imagine the linoleum floors being gritty and the glasses brought out to the customers not being entirely clean. But the color in the film was dark, so the impression of dirt could have been simply from the shadowiness of the film quality.

Violet went around, pouring coffee, chatting with this urban cowboy, then that one. Because of the apron she didn't seem naked most of the time. You only knew she was naked when she turned around.

Eventually she sat with a cowboy near the jukebox. The cowboy was younger than the others and handsome in an innocent way. He looked like a high school student from some hilly Iowa town who'd arrived in New York only a week before. In contrast, Violet looked like a figure from a pre-Raphaelite painting. Her skin was strikingly pale. Her curly red hair was parted in the middle and cascaded wildly to her shoulders.

The conversation between her and the cowboy lasted several minutes. Everyone in Frank's living room remained quiet, as if they could hear the words, or as if they could read the lips. Then there was a cut and a new scene. Now the film showed Violet and the cowboy in an apartment with peeling walls and a pigeon fluttering around near the bed. Violet and the cowboy were on a naked mattress, the cowboy sprawled on his stomach and Violet removing a hypodermic needle from a briefcase. They remained naked. Violet no longer wore the apron, though she now wore a pair of black lace gloves, and the cowboy had removed the hat but not the bandanna.

She climbed on top of the cowboy, the needle in her hand. She sat on his back and slapped his ass a few times very hard and his feet wiggled and then she lifted her hand. She plunged the needle into his rump. His toes curled. Then they slowly uncurled. Violet looked up, at the camera, at the viewer, at us.

The film stopped. Frank turned off the projector and switched on a lamp and clapped, the cigarette dangling from his lip.

"Does it make you jealous, Frank?" Violet asked from the sofa.

"Me? No, dear. I'm a modern man, with a modern sense of discretion about these matters. Also, having you shove a needle in my ass has never been a fantasy of mine."

"You're probably right. I bet there's a few hundred other items on your list before you'd get to that one."

Juanita looked over at Violet. "This is the second time I've seen it. The first time was with you in New York and that one had sound. The second time is tonight, with Dad playing the Bach. Tell Andy when you see him he should get rid of the dialogue and put in the Bach instead. The dialogue is horrible. All that talk about the nature of steak."

"I don't think Andy likes Bach," Violet told her. "I don't think he likes music, period. Silence is more his thing."

"But if he adds the Bach, he elevates the film and degrades the music," Juanita replied. "And they end up meeting somewhere in between."

"You should tell him yourself," Violet responded. "You haven't come up for a visit in ages."

"I got robbed last time I was there, remember? And the son of a bitch hit me in the face before he ran away."

"As if there weren't any muggings in Memphis," Violet said.

"There's plenty. I just haven't been victim of one yet."

"So you admit your fear of New York is arbitrary."

"It's utterly fucking arbitrary."

Freddie, the junkie, rose from his chair in the corner and scratched at his thick beard. His hands looked like they had not been washed in days. "Well, I thought the movie was great," he said. "It's about mythology. It's about bringing the American gods down from their Texas mountainsides and throwing them into dirty little diners. It's about the word made flesh."

"Fuck you," Juanita said cheerfully. "That was not what it was about at all. And remember, I've seen it twice."

Violet rose and crossed the room and placed an arm around Frank's neck and took his cigarette from his mouth and inhaled from it and placed it back in Frank's mouth. "It was made years ago anyway," she said. "When I watch it now all I think of is my youth."

"What year was it made?" Oscar asked.

"Either in the last months of the sixties or the first months of the seventies," she said. "It was a confusing time. Hippies were losing their innocence. Vietnam was losing its novelty."

"I don't remember that time at all," Freddie said. "I don't think I was born yet." Oscar looked at him, not knowing what to make of this. Freddie was clearly decades older than himself.

"Because you were born yesterday, and you'll die tomorrow," Juanita said, again in a cheerful voice. She took after her father, having a dark complexion, as if she were southern Italian even though she was not. Frank's family was English, having arrived in the Mississippi Delta in the late eighteenth century. She looked over at Violet. "Who was the cowboy?"

"You want me to introduce you to him when you come up?"

"I don't usually like cowboys but I liked him."

Frank said, "Maybe you two should discuss this in another room."

"Daddy doesn't like me hanging out with cowboys," said Juanita.

"The queer ones I don't mind you seeing. It's the straight ones I don't trust. All those pseudo-John Wayne types have something up the sleeve. They've made a mockery of the noble cowherd. John Wayne was made of granite. He never had an erotic thought in his life. All he cared about was beans, bad coffee, taking land from Mexican peasants, and Texas sky."

Four

Oscar and Juanita spoke in the den. Violet and Frank had gone upstairs where a record by Johnny Ace was now blasting. Freddie had shot up and was now on the sofa in the corner of the den, eyes shut and lips in a slight smile. Oscar and Juanita sat across from one another in large leather chairs. "I keep thinking about Tommy," she said. "I hope he's in a better place, though I'm not sure I entirely believe it."

"That he's in a better place?"

"That a better place exists."

Oscar leaned back, crossing his legs. "I expect wherever he is it can't be any worse than where he was when he was alive."

"You really think that?"

"I do. I think he was miserable. And it wasn't the drugs that made him miserable. It was the misery that led him to the drugs. Not that they made it any better. He was always rushing around, trying to scrounge up enough change for his next fix. I'd rather be a street dog than live that way. Christ."

"Speaks he who has probably tried everything that can be smoked, swallowed, or injected at least once in his life."

"Yeah, but I don't make a regular diet of it. I've tried heroin twice to see what all the fuss is about. I don't feel much need to try it again." Oscar gestured toward Freddie, who was snoring, his head cradled in his arm. "That's never going to be me."

"Well, lucky you." She rose and went to the bar between the two long windows black with night and fixed more cocktails. Oscar looked down at his hands and saw they were trembling slightly. Oscar said, "I need to ask you something."

"All right."

"Back a few weeks ago you said you got a letter from him."

"Yeah, I told you all about it."

"Can you tell me again? I wasn't listening that closely."

"Of course you weren't." She handed him a White Russian. "It wasn't a letter, it was a newspaper clipping. It was about that city council guy, the one who killed himself. It was his obituary."

"I remember that guy. I remember hearing about his death on the news."

"It was a few days before Christmas. He went out to the shed behind his house with his pistol."

"And shot himself?"

"No, hanged himself. He just took the gun out there to clean it. Yes, Oscar, he shot himself."

"You have the clipping?"

"Someplace in my apartment. I think I do at least."

"Can I see it?"

"Right now? It's two in the morning."

"You weren't planning on going home at some point?"

"Not at two in the morning, and not with all the drinks I've had. I still have my old room upstairs."

"I'll drive. I'm not that bad off."

They took his black Chevrolet Chevelle, what some of his friends called his pimpmobile. Back in the mid-sixties, he'd been in a group called the Toy Soldiers that had a string of nationwide hits. This was before he knew Tommy and before they formed Cosmic Dust. Oscar had been the lead singer in the band and they'd toured across the U.S. and even had a few shows in England. He'd been incredibly young: sixteen, seventeen. This car, this long black automobile he loved, had been paid for with the little money he'd had leftover from his Toy Soldiers days. Nothing else remained. He'd lived off of the money for a few years but one morning he woke up and realized it was all gone, spent on drinks for himself and friends and fancy guitars and plane rides around the country.

Juanita lived in an apartment building on Cleveland Avenue, across the street from Crump Stadium. The place was yellow-brick with a red tile roof, and it had a shrub-filled courtyard that lent it a Spanish air. They pulled up into the parking lot. In the center of it someone had thrown a glass bottle, leaving a star of glass shards, and the cars in the lot were parked away from it. Oscar did too, parking near a dumpster with a cock spray-painted on it.

Inside her apartment Juanita rummaged through the shoeboxes under her bed. Oscar walked around in a circle and drank from a bottle of Budwieser. "Found it," she said.

"Thanks." He took the slip of paper and sat on the bed. She sat next to him. They read it. His name had been Edward Parker and his father had been mayor of Memphis back in the forties. Edward the son had been on the city council for fifteen years. He left behind a wife and a son who went to Ole Miss. The picture at the top of the obituary showed a man with neatly combed white hair and large cheekbones. Oscar turned the slip of paper over and saw part of an advertisement for a Sony television. But at the bottom of the paper Tommy had written a few words in blue ink, the letters cramped and hardly legible. One line read I did this and the other one said I was not alone and the others they shall find me.

Oscar brought the paper away from his face. "You didn't tell me he wrote some shit on the back."

"It was so small I never bothered to read it. I still can't read it. What does it say?"

"It says you need to get your eyes checked."

"Oscar."

He told her. Then he placed the slip of paper on the bed between them. They remained still and the wind blew through the open balcony doors and stirred the edges of the checkered cloth on the table near those doors.

Juanita asked, "So what's the story? You think this has any deeper meaning than Tommy doing some weird shit while stoned one day?"

"He send you any other newspaper clippings?"

"That was the only one. It's the only thing I got from him after he moved out west."

"You ever talk to him on the phone?"

She nodded no. She pointed to the slip of newspaper on the bed. "That was the last communiqué." She added, "I have to admit, I got this in the mail and glanced at it and didn't think about it again until right now."

Oscar stood and walked in a circle again and rubbed the back of his neck. "Something is going on."

"And what do you think that might be?"

"I have this negative vibe about the whole damn thing, Juanita. Look at my hands. They've been like this for days."

He showed them to her. They were trembling slightly. She looked up. "You don't think it was an overdose."

"I think it might have been an overdose. That's what the cops said and I guess they'd know. But I think there was more going on too."

"You think he was killed?"

"I don't know if I'd go that far. I just think we don't have the entire story. I told you about that time he called not long ago. I think they're messages. I think they're Tommy trying to say something he didn't want to put into words. I think he was afraid to put it into words but I don't know why." He added, "As soon as Brian called me up and told me Tommy had died, I felt it was wrong somehow. It's hard to explain, but I feel it all over and it hasn't left me for a second. It's more than the call and it's more than that obituary. There's something about this that won't leave me alone."

Juanita stood from the bed and walked out the balcony doors and placed her hand on the metal railing. Oscar followed her. They looked into the courtyard where a cat bathed itself at the foot of a stone birdbath, its tail in its paws. A white dogwood petal floated in the water of the birdbath. It would be dawn in two or three hours. She said, "Let's see Grace."

"You think we should? They broke up a while back."

"She was closer to him than we were. She might know something. If nothing else he might've sent her messages from Tucson too."

Five

At first Liz couldn't see them as they approached. The sun was too bright. She raised her hand over her eyes and only then did she see them. They walked over the gravel in front of the house. There were three of them and they were all men. The oldest one had gray hair and a cardigan and a blue shirt buttoned to his neck and the two on either side of him wore black pants and white shirts with the sleeves rolled to their elbows. One of the two held carried a briefcase. The other carried a milkshake in a paper cup.

Beside her Horace was sitting on the top porch step, wearing a pair of gold-frame sunglasses.

The oldest one was named Vince. Horace had told her about him. "Pretty little bit of country you have out here," he said when he stood a few feet from the porch.

"We don't own the place," Horace said. "We borrow it sometimes."

"But it's safe? It's an okay place for us?"

"Yeah. The guy who owns it, Jimmy, he's a good guy. He's almost deaf and not that quick but he's helped us a lot over the years."

"He here now?" the guy with the milkshake asked. He started looking up at the second story windows.

"He's in his room," Liz told them. "He won't bother us."

"And he's half deaf so he won't hear us if we speak in a normal tone of voice, is that right?" Vince said.

Horace smiled. "He makes it his business to stay ignorant

of most things. Even he wasn't almost deaf we wouldn't have to worry."

Vince glanced at the man with the briefcase. "Cold you find this man and ask him to go on a short constitutional?" To Horace and Liz, he asked, "You mind?"

"He'd be fine with that, I reckon," Liz said.

The man with the briefcase without a word climbed the porch steps and entered the house and soon they could hear his steps on the staircase inside. "He really is okay, though," Horace told Vince. "I'm careful about this shit."

"I like to be a little more than careful," Vince said, removing his fedora and fanning his head. He had a rigid posture and a wide chest and despite his age he looked hard and young. Jimmy came out on to the porch, a baseball cap low over his eyes. He did not look at anyone. He strode from the porch into the line of pines about fifty feet to the west of the house as if he were alone on his property.

Vince watched Jimmy. Then he turned to Liz, walking up to her with his hand extended. "Horace says you're quite the busy bee."

"We make good partners most of the time."

They shook hands. He said, "Good to finally meet you, Liz. Unlike some of my associates, I believe in having more women in our ranks. The wider our lines of activity, the better."

They drank ice tea around the kitchen table. Vince told them how well certain neighborhoods in New Orleans were doing. "America's going down the piss-hole," he said, "but it's good for business." The two younger men barely said a word. One looked at Liz during the meeting and winked and Liz smiled and turned her head back to Vince. It was warm for April even by the standards of Choctaw County, Mississippi, and flies buzzed around the ceiling and hovered around the screen door.

After twenty minutes, Vince said, "I was under the impression another one was supposed to be here. Why is he not here?"

"He tends to run behind," Liz said.

"I really want to acquaint myself with some of your people, Horace. That was one of the reasons I came up this way. I don't travel for the scenery, lovely though it may be."

Horace nodded. He still wore his sunglasses. "You want some more tea, Vince?"

"My doctor would say I shouldn't. Not with all that sugar you've got in it. But he's not here so fuck him."

Horace stood and opened the refrigerator door and removed the glass bottle of tea and poured it into everyone's glasses. Liz saw Vince smiling, the first time he'd smiled this afternoon. A loud rumbling truck pulled up outside. The smell of it drifted through the windows. She could hear Max get out from the truck and raise the hood. She heard him curse to himself. "That would be him," Liz assured Vince.

"Very good. Very good." Vince took a handkerchief from the pocket of his cardigan, blew his nose, and placed it back in his pocket. "Horace, sit back down. We need to discuss something."

Liz looked at Horace and he looked at her and raised an eyebrow slightly and sat next to her at the table. Vince said, "I'm getting to be an old man and I know that doesn't make me wise but it has given me a certain amount of experience in how to handle a range of situations."

He ran his hand through his thick gray hair. Then he placed both hands on the table, interlacing his fingers. "I get the sense at times that there is a certain laxness going on up here."

Horace said, "There's not, Vince. About eighty percent of the stuff on the streets right now, it comes through us. Not the pot, but the harder shit."

"This so?" said one of the younger men. He still held his milkshake. He took a sip from the straw.

"Sure is," Liz said.

Vince turned to her. "There was recently a situation with some bikers. I believe they were from Texas. Could you speak briefly about that, Liz?"

She tried to speak to everyone at the table and not simply Vince, whose eyes bored into her. She said, "Some bikers moved up here around Christmas. They came up from Houston and bought this house in a black neighborhood off Lamar, near the Stax studio. They made their presence in the neighborhood known pretty quickly by really fucking up the house. They put plastic garbage bags over the windows and had this lizard skeleton hanging on the porch and they nailed up a couple of dozen BEWARE OF DOG signs up on the walls of the place. So they did that, trying to show they meant business, I guess. And then they started selling in the area. Mostly PCP and Quaaludes and Tuinal at first, then they were dealing coke and heroin. But they weren't professionals. They were just some guys trying to make an extra buck. They did have a supply line coming up from Mexico into Texas, or so I've heard through the grapevine, but it didn't run deep. Anyway, shit they were selling was low quality crap, but it was cheaper too, so you can imagine the demand. They didn't try to expand, though. I think they wanted to make enough to buy food and more motorcycles or whatever but that was it. It wasn't some grand vision."

"How long were they selling?" asked the man with the milkshake.

Liz glanced at Horace. She said, "A few months."

"And why exactly did you wait so long to handle these gentleman from Houston?" asked Vince, folding his arms across his chest.

Horace spoke up. "Rumor was some of the guys had a link with the police here. The bikers themselves claimed it. We heard this from some of the customers."

"So you just believed it?" Vince stared at him coolly.

"Considering how some of the police are these days, yeah. I mean, we wanted to check it out. And we did. And we eventually found out it was a load of bullshit. But that was one of the reasons it took a while to deal with these assholes."

Liz added, "Max and me, we dealt with them too. They left

town bleeding and moaning and limping and some were even missing a few parts. They're going to give Memphis a wide berth from here on out."

The screen door opened and Max stepped in wearing jeans with holes in both knees and a Led Zeppelin T-shirt. "Nice of you to join us, young man," Vince said, not turning his head.

"I had truck trouble. Damn thing needs a new engine but I finally got it going enough to get my ass over here. Though soon as I took the keys out all this goddamn smoke started pouring out from under the hood." His eyes scanned everyone at the table. "How're yall doing? Hot as shit for this time of year."

He held out his hand to Vince and Vince remained still, only shifting and taking the hand after several seconds passed. As he shook Max's hand he looked up at Max's face. "What the hell did you do to your hand? Looks like you have the stigmata?"

Max threw a glance over towards Liz and Horace and held out his other hand for Vince to see. "They match," he said. Then he told Vince, "Back a few years ago I got in some trouble because I was selling shit where somebody else wanted to sell the same shit. So to scare me they took me out and nailed my arms to a plank of wood."

"They crucified you?" asked Vince.

"They didn't do my feet so I'm not sure if you could call it a full crucifixion. I guess you called call it half of one though."

Vince smiled at Horace and then Liz. "You play rough up here in Choctaw County, Mississippi."

"I'm from Memphis," Max told him.

He shrugged. "Okay. Memphis."

The young man with the milkshake stood, leaving the cup on the table. He reached down and took something from his boot and when he rose Liz could see it was a knife about four inches long with a shiny black handle. He jabbed it into Max's side three hard times and the two of them grunted together with each jab. Liz placed the palm of her hand over her mouth. Horace bolted up, his chair falling behind his legs, and walked back until he was against the kitchen cabinet. The young man held Max as Max lost strength in his legs. Max said, "You fucking fucker you."

"Should've been on time, Max," said the man holding him.

Vince kept his eyes on Horace and Liz and said, "I'll explain in a moment. You two are fine. You two have not a thing to worry about."

The other young man stood and the two grabbed Max by his shoulders and one of them kicked open the screen door and then they were dragging Max outside as Max screamed and pleaded. The screen door slammed shut. There were grunt sounds out in the yard. Then it was quiet and Liz could hear the flies buzzing overhead. "Can I have another glass of tea?" Vince asked Horace. Liz stood, feeling she had to do something, sensing that if she did not move she would begin to shake all over. She was suddenly freezing despite the warm breeze coming through the door and windows. "I'll get it," she managed to say.

"This was about letting something fester," Vince explained. "If a group of idiot biker boys from Texas move into an area that is rightfully ours you do not take that casually. If you were concerned about the MPD situation you find out what the true situation is and rectify it. You do not take weeks on these matters, much less months. The one thing we've always had going for us is speed."

Horace nodded, his hands gripping the counter behind him. His face had drawn into itself as if every ounce of flesh had dried up into bone.

Liz placed the tea in front of Vince. She said, "Can I say something in our defense?"

"You are not on trial here. But go on, yeah."

"The day we got one of the cops to tell us these bikers were full of shit regarding that cop connection, we moved in. We were all over them. That place was a house of horrors for a night. And after they left town we paid some local kids to burn the place down. We pulverized them."

"This isn't about your abilities. I have faith in those. What I don't have faith in is your sense of urgency." Vince glanced at her and drank from the tea very slowly and placed the glass on the table and wiped his lips with a napkin. "Tasty drink, Liz," he said. "Very tasty."

The screen door opened. One of the young guys stuck his head in. There were splotches of blood on his white shirt. He asked where the shovels were and Liz said the garage and he winked at her again and closed the door. Vince said, "Like I said, you two have nothing to worry about. The demonstration is over. I hope you learned your lesson, though. You cannot let things fester."

Horace picked his chair up and sat down, droplets of sweat on his nose and his forehead. He said, "Why Max though?"

"You think I don't have eyes down there? You think when I'm in New Orleans or hanging out in Miami I can't see Memphis and Mississippi with my telescope? Max was not reliable. He's late to meetings and he skims off the top in some deals and he bad mouths you and the lady here at parties and get-togethers." He touched the back of his ear. "I've got people and those people have people. Now we are not Gestapo. We're not Soviet thugs who don't trust their own people. But when a certain somebody gets out of hand, starts stealing more than would be reasonably acceptable or bad mouthing friends, we do hear about it." He made a slight shrug. "Gossip is not that bad of a thing altogether. It has its place in this world we've made for ourselves."

Vince finished his tea and stood and stared down at his cardigan. He removed a piece of lint with his fingertips and brushed his hands together and the lint fell to the floor. "I'm not cruel. None of us are cruel. But we have to cover our asses. You two weren't around back in the sixties when that little Kennedy fucker was after us. We pushed back hard, real hard, and he finally decided to move on to other things."

Liz could hear the shovels digging outside. It sounded far from the house yet she could hear them. She knew she would hear it again tonight in bed just as she heard the wails of some of the people she beat and hurt in bed and she already saw herself staring at the ceiling and rubbing her fingers in her scalp and praying to the God she did not believe in to help her relax, to help her fall backwards into sleep, and the God she did not believe in would say nothing, do nothing, and simply watch her through the ceiling from the home in the sky in which he did not live.

Vince moved over toward the kitchen door, placing his hands in his pockets. Standing there, he looked like a retired schoolteacher or accountant with an extensive cardigan collection at home. "No more guys like Max and no more letting bikers from Texas get away with shit." He turned, shaking his head as if tired of this trip and the entire day.

"Okay," Horace said.

"Message delivered," Liz added.

Vince laughed. "Bikers are even worse than fucking hippies. At least the hippies have a charm about them. The few that remain with us, I mean. Seems like most of them have taken their flowers out their hair and they're pretty much like anybody else these days."

After the three men from New Orleans left, Liz and Horace took a bottle of Jim Beam out from the cabinet by the sink, where Jimmy kept his liquor. They didn't talk. Horace cleared his voice as if about to speak but then said nothing. As they were sipping their second drinks Jimmy stepped in through the door. He spoke in a whisper, saying. "I don't think you two should be using this property anymore." He took off his dingy baseball cap and wiped his eyes and placed his cap back on his head.

Horace glared up at him, his hands tight around his glass. "We pay you real good, Jimmy, and this place has a certain convenience for us."

Jimmy nodded.

"You don't like being ordered out of your own house, do you?" Liz asked. She used the tone she employed when talking to small children.

"It's not right, then telling me to get out of my own house like that. Shit."

Horace stood and squeezed Jimmy's shoulders and brought his close and embraced him. "We need you, man. You know that? We like you. We respect you. Those guys today you'll probably never have to see again."

"The thing about you, Jimmy," Liz added, looking up at his from where she was sitting, "is that you and me and Horace are all working on the same side of things. We don't want no regular job, right? We probably couldn't do one if we tried. People like us, people who try to find their own way, people like that have to stick together, Jimmy."

He nodded again. He looked at her and pushed back the bill of his cap and muttered, "Shit."

There was no moon and no stars and as Liz drove the white van down the curved gravel drive leading from Jimmy's grounds to the main road branches would appear low over the windshield and then rattle along the roof of the van. In the darkness behind them they'd left Jimmy boiling some hot dogs in his kitchen and Max under a pine about sixty yards from the front porch. She and Horace had walked out to where they'd heard shoveling before getting in the van. Liz had crossed herself, standing near the upturned earth, and Horace knelt by it and touched it and stood and wiped his fingers against the thigh of his jeans. In the van riding back to Memphis, Liz said, "I don't know, Horace. I really don't."

"Don't know?"

"This whole thing, it's not the thrill it used to be. When we got together, it was exciting. Now it's something else."

"We both liked Max but let's not kid ourselves. I bet Max couldn't whistle and tie his shoes at the same time if his life depended on it."

"So you think it was right, what went down this afternoon?"

"Not even a little."

"Sounds like you do."

"I'm trying to explain the situation from Vince's point of view."

"You think Max was skimming shit off the top?"

Horace flicked his cigarette through the window. "I wouldn't put it past him. When he was working with some of Vince's guys over in Orange Mound, yeah, I could see him doing it thinking everybody does it a little."

"Max did not deserve that."

"You do remember you nailed his hands to a plank of wood, right?"

"He changed since that night. For years he did us good."

"I don't like it either, Liz. But as long as we're careful I think the two of us will keep doing okay. Vince implied as much."

"But how can we know? After what Vince did, I don't see how we can feel safe around him again."

"I think something about Max must've set him off. I think there might be some shit we aren't even aware of."

"And if there's not? Horace, he could've beaten the shit out of Max, he could've knocked him around so hard he'd never look the same again, he could've done a whole lot of shit before doing what he did today. That's all I have to say about it."

Horace touched her elbow. "I'm not sitting over here disagreeing with you. I liked the dude too."

They arrived in Memphis as rain started to fall and soon it was blowing across the road in huge gusty sheets. The traffic lights on Lamar Avenue danced on their wires above the splattering asphalt. They passed pawnshops and motels and a cemetery and Graceland, where Elvis had died the previous summer. The night of the death she'd driven by in her van, looking at the mourners and the cops watching over the mourners. She'd liked Elvis. She didn't like his music so much but she liked him and how he dressed in those shiny space-age jumpsuits and his hair. David Bowie was always trying to act like a space alien but Elvis Presley seemed damn near to being the real thing.

Liz let Horace out at a Ralph's Pizza on Summer Avenue, where he'd left his '67 Buick, and continued driving west toward Overton Park. There was a small apartment building across the street from the park on its eastern side, a two-story rectangle of maybe twenty apartments. Liz walked up the metal steps to the second floor landing and knocked on the door at the end of that landing. She removed her cap, ran her hand through her hair. The door opened and Richard looked surprised, standing in his jockey shorts and black Sex Pistols T-shirt, only one feeble lamp on in the room behind him. "You never call," he said. "Just once I'd like to not be surprised."

"But you like surprises."

"On occasion. Not every single moment of my life though."

In the kitchen he made a pot of coffee. There were dirty plates in the sink, a smeared cockroach corpse on the wall by the phone. He asked why she looked so upset. "I look upset?" she asked.

He nodded and slid a hand under his big T-shirt and scratched his belly. He weighed about a hundred and twenty pounds. He was bone and a little muscle and a spiky head of hair and nothing more.

"It's none of your business why I'm upset," she told him. "It would scare the hell out of you anyway."

"I'm not scared so easily." He poured their coffee.

"Bullshit. You can listen to all the Sid Vicious you want, you still scare easy."

"You like to mistake me for somebody else, Liz."

"You were born in Germantown to a doctor and a doctor's wife. You rode horses and your prom was at that swanky club downtown."

"That ain't my life now. Not one bit."

He sat across from her and placed one foot on the inner part of her calf and slid it up slowly until it reached her inner thigh. She drank her coffee, felt his foot press between her legs. He was right. He was not that boy he talked about after

37

they made love or after he shot up. Richard hung out in Overton Park some afternoons in his snug leather jacket and got picked up by guys who'd pay him for a blowjob and he'd take his earnings and spend it on coke, on heroin, on pills. His parents turned their back to him about a year ago. At one time he'd had a beautiful sister but she'd died of an overdose in a shithole shack in the Uptown area of Chicago in the early seventies. His parents refused to go through that ordeal again. They turned their backs on him. They made it so he was already dead to them. That way when he did die the shock would not be as catastrophic as it had been with his sister. She sipped. The coffee tasted burnt. She'd never had a cup of coffee in this kitchen that didn't taste burnt. "It's still a matter of how you grew up," she said. Her voice was softer. "It's what you see when your mind is still forming. You might think you're some tough son of a bitch punk but I know all I have to do is scratch the surface and there's a scared little Germantown boy underneath."

"Try me, you fat cunt."

She placed the mug on the table. She stood and grabbed him by the back of his neck and led him into the bedroom. She threw him on the mattress on his stomach and removed her belt and tied his hands with it. She turned him over, grabbed the waistband of his jockey shorts, and yanked them down to his knees. Richard breathed hard. He breathed like an excited dog. From the top drawer in the bureau she took out more belts and a spanking board and a pair of brass knuckles and a dog collar and leather leash. "You ready for me to start scratching?" she said, turning toward him.

He leaned back, his shoulders against the headboard, and raised his feet, waiting to be tied.

"Liz, with you there's not a moment when I'm not ready," he told her.

She smacked his bare hip with the board with such force he let out a whimper. "I saw a friend killed today," she told him. "I saw him stabbed right in front of me."

Richard turned to her, his teeth wet, saliva in the corners

of his mouth. "I bet you had somebody do it."

She smacked his side again. "I did not."

"I just bet you did. You always have your filthy hand in something."

She turned him over and held him hard against the mattress by gripping his hair and pushing his head into the pillow. As she struck his ass over and over again with the board he whimpered and laughed and whimpered again.

"You make me sick with myself," she said, continuing to strike him.

Red welts appeared on his skinny ass. "Please," he said.

"What did you say?"

"Please. Please stop for a minute. I'm going get sick if you don't."

She threw the paddled across the room, got up from the mattress. She lit a cigarette and looked around. The air in the bedroom smelled of dirty socks and dried semen and Coke and French fries. There was only one poster on the wall: Steve McQueen in a turtleneck and bomber jacket, smoking a cigarette. She stepped toward his image and smiled and blew smoke up at his face.

"Tell me when you're ready," she said.

Six

There were hydrangeas growing under the front porch of the bungalow and strips of creeping phlox flanking the stone steps leading to the lawn. A low hedge separated Grace's yard from the yard next door, where a plastic kid pool set in the sunlight. Two girls of about eight or nine splashed in its water.

Oscar asked, "You ever do anything like this before?"

"What kind of life do you think I live?" Juanita answered.

"I'm only asking." He glanced out the passenger window. "Shit, I'm not even sure what we should be looking for. She's going to think it's weird, us just showing up to talk with her."

"Yeah, but can you think of any other way?"

"No, I can't."

Oscar continued staring through the car window at the house. Grace lived there with her mother. Juanita had phoned her the previous day. She barely knew Grace though she had spoken with her at a few bars over the years. She asked Grace if she could stop by to ask her a few questions about Tommy. Grace had seemed hesitant. She paused, asked what type of questions. Oscar had been standing next to Juanita in Juanita's kitchen and had heard the conversation. Juanita had said she'd rather speak with her in person about the matter. Grace finally said yes. Oscar could hear her voice speaking in the phone. It was terse. It was suspicious. She had reasons to be when you considered she and Tommy hadn't been together since January, and it was now April. What kind of questions could Juanita possibly have?

They were on Avalon Street, a few houses north of Jackson Boulevard. As she opened her door, Juanita said, "You notice something?"

"Probably."

"You notice how this isn't a white neighborhood?"

"Well, Grace herself isn't white."

"She's not? I had no idea."

"Tommy told me. After they were dating for a while she had him over for dinner, with her mother. That was when he realized."

"What did Tommy think?"

"I think he was turned on by the idea of dating a black woman. He didn't say that but I could tell from the way he talked."

"Yeah, a gorgeous woman who looks Italian. How politically radical of him."

"We should go in. If she sees us, she's going to start wondering why we're sitting here. She might think we're afraid to get out of the car."

"It's not a dangerous neighborhood."

"I know, I know."

Oscar had cleaned himself up for the visit. He wore a spotless white shirt and he had wetted and combed back his thick curly hair. According to Tommy, Grace's mother was devout and somewhat old-fashioned. Pictures of Jesus and Moses and Abraham hung through the house and she'd told Tommy at dinner that he would be a more handsome young man if he simply cut his hair shorter.

Grace answered the door before they rang the bell. "You two sat in that car long enough," she said.

She had black eyes and black ringlets that fell to her shoulder. Tommy said she'd been a model in San Francisco. When her mother was diagnosed a year ago with dementia she returned to Memphis to help take care of her. "I'm sorry about that," Oscar said to her. "We were listening to a song on the radio we really liked."

Grace led them into the living room where a woman in a pink housecoat was eating lunch on a TV tray. The television played in front of her, the volume turned up high. Grace squatted next to her mother and touched her shoulder and said, "Mama, these are the people I told you were going to drop by. Remember when I said that this morning, how there were people coming by? I'm going to speak with them in the kitchen."

Her mother picked up a milk carton and drank from the straw. She placed the carton on the corner of the tray and stiffly turned her neck and said, "What do they want? They want something with me?"

"No, Mama. With me. They're going to ask me some questions."

"You in trouble?" She stared at Oscar.

"Not at all, Mama. We're going to be in the kitchen for a minute."

"All right then. Good to meet you." She smiled up at Oscar and Juanita and they smiled back.

The kitchen was in the back of the house down a long hallway and it was surprisingly big, with a high ceiling and lime-green walls. Grace did not offer them anything to drink. She sat at the table and they sat at the table across from her. "I never knew you two were related. So you're cousins?"

"On my mother's side," Oscar told her. "My uncle is her father. My mom is her aunt."

"You don't look a thing alike."

"I think we probably got two very different sets of genes," Juanita said. "I'm from the part of the family that for some reason looks Italian."

"And you're not?"

"No. English."

"People think I look Italian too. Or Spanish. I once had a boyfriend who used to call me his gypsy queen. I'm not any of those things. At least that I know of. It's peculiar how when white people meet a black woman who's a little bit light-skinned they invent this exotic history about her. Instead of thinking about what probably really happened to make her look so pale." She leaned forward. "So what is this about? You were vague over the phone. I mean, you do realize we broke up back in January, right? I don't know anything about Tommy's last days, if that's what you came over here for. And I'm guessing it is because I can't think of another reason why you two would be here."

Juanita took a deep breath. "I don't know how to really begin. That's why I was being vague."

"Just start somewhere," Grace said.

Juanita crossed her legs and placed her hands on her knee. She said there was something off about Tommy's death. She told Grace about the phone call Tommy had given Oscar and about the clipping from the newspaper she had received. "It's intuition, what we're going on here," she concluded, "but we were wondering, since you were his last serious girlfriend, if you have any information that might help us."

"Even something small," added Oscar. "Even that would help us out."

"I didn't get any mysterious messages like you two did, I'll tell you that. After he left Memphis I never heard from him again. When we broke up we kept in touch a little: just a phone call now and then. I don't know why we did it since we both knew we weren't ever going to get back together." She stood and took a bottle of Tab from the refrigerator and poured a glass by the sink. "The breakup wasn't exactly a smooth one. There was a certain amount of bitterness toward the end."

"Could we ask you why?" Oscar said.

"I don't see how it would help."

"Anything would help," Juanita told her.

"Mostly it was the drugs. I was getting sick of it. I'm not going to stand here and act like I haven't snorted some coke and swallowed some pills off and on through the years. That's stopped now, especially with my mom being how she is at this point, but when I used to live in San Francisco and the first few months I was back here in Memphis, I used to enjoy a good party as much as anyone. But Tommy wasn't using drugs to party anymore. He was using them to wake up in the morning. He was using them to go to bed at night. I had an uncle like that. He'd vanish, and then come around our house once a year, usually around Christmas, asking for money. He was in deep, and Tommy, I thought, was getting in just as deep." She took a sip and looked over at them. She eyed them skeptically. "If you two are playing detective, shouldn't you all be writing this down? Isn't that what they do in the movies?"

Oscar looked at Juanita. He mouthed, "I don't have anything to write with." Juanita went through her purse. She took out a memo pad. She dug around further into her purse. "All right, I guess I'll help you out," Grace said. There was a mason jar of pens and pencils setting next to the coffeemaker. She took a pen, she handed it to Juanita.

"It was mainly the drugs?" asked Juanita. "That was why you two broke up?"

Grace swept her hair back and twisted it into a bun. "Like I said, mostly. But there was this other reason. It was the last goddamn straw for me, regarding him. One day, he said he was out with a friend, and this friend would drop him off here, and we'd get dinner someplace. I said sure, that sounded good. He got here right when he said he would, he wasn't late. But the person driving him here, she did not look like a friend."

"You mean she looked like someone he might be seeing?"

"No, I don't mean that. Tommy and I, we weren't exclusive, you know? We saw other people occasionally too. It wasn't a bit deal. No, he was in this white Volkswagen van, and the driver of that van was this fat white chick in a leather jacket and cap, kind of like the cap police wear. I was looking out the window at them though they didn't see me. She was talking, this white girl. She was speaking very firmly, almost as if she were a teacher and Tommy this student who was always in trouble. She was poking him in the chest with her finger and he was just nodding and nodding. He had what I would call a tortured look on his face: he clearly did not like what she was saying."

"And you don't think they were dating?" Oscar asked.

"No. When Tommy and I got into an argument, he never looked like that. Not like he looked with that woman. When Tommy and I argued, we argued, you know? We were engaged, we were looking each other in the eye. What was going on with Tommy in that van was entirely different, there's no doubt in my mind about that. He could barely look over at that woman. The argument was a one-way street. All her and no him."

Grace's mother started calling from the living room. She repeated her name over and over, Gracie, Gracie, Gracie I need you. Grace left the kitchen. Oscar turned to Juanita, rubbing his cheek. "What are we even doing here? We're not detectives."

"We could always give up. But you know and I know there's something more to the story."

Oscar nodded. "I took off work today to do this. That's fifty-five dollars I won't be getting paid."

"You really should try to find a better line of work."

"Music is my line of work."

"And how many bills has that been paying recently?"

Grace stepped back into the room with a damp dishtowel in her hand. She squeezed it over the sink and placed it over the neck of the faucet and returned to the table. When Oscar would see her with Tommy she was usually smiling and laughing and talking about what she and her friends had done the night before and what they might do the night after. She would talk about how much she missed San Francisco and she'd talk about her different trips to New York. The somber woman he was seeing today he had never seen before. He realized the other Grace was alive too: she simply wasn't here in this kitchen today. When she sat back at the table, she said, "Ya'll are going have to leave in a few minutes. Mama takes an afternoon nap and I have to help get her in bed."

"Would you mind finishing the story before we go?" Oscar asked.

"Story?"

"About the fat lady in the van."

"That's right, yeah. Well, when Tommy came inside we got into this argument about her. Mama was asleep in the back so she didn't hear it. And my aunt, who was coming over to watch Mama while I was out, hadn't gotten here yet. I'm glad because it was one of our worst arguments. Tommy came in and I could tell right away he was in one of his moods and I could also tell that he was upset about something the woman in the van had said. I asked him about it. I asked him who she was and why he'd been with her. And he said he didn't want to talk about it. Then I asked again." She smiled. "I can be real persistent. And he told me if I didn't stop nagging him about it he was going to walk out the door. So I did ask him about it again. I told him if he was in some kind of trouble, I needed to know about it. I told him I was tired of feeling like some girl he just took out to dinner and fucked every few nights. If we were ever going to get more serious, he had to open up more. Well, Tommy stood up and looked like he was going to hit his fist against the wall. He looked as angry as I ever saw him. And as desperate too. But he didn't hit the wall. He shook himself the way a cat shakes itself when it gets wet and he walked out the door. It'd started to rain but it didn't seem to bother him. He walked down the street with the rain pouring down on him."

"That the last time you saw him?" asked Juanita.

"I saw him a few more times. But it was pretty much dead between us by then. I never even bothered to bring up the fat white chick again. I figured, what was the point?"

Oscar shook his head. "Tommy never told me what happened between you two. I'd ask and he'd act like it had never been that serious between you to begin with."

"It got close to the point of getting serious. Then it rapidly

---

46

moved back away from that."

Juanita asked, "And when did that afternoon take place? That afternoon you saw him in the white van?"

"Well, that was the day we pretty much broke up. It would've been late January, so about two and a half months ago." Her mother called from the living room again. Gracie, Gracie, come here, dear, I finished my milk. Grace said to them, "Time for you all to go. I have to get Mama in bed."

She led them through the long hallway. As the three of them stood on the porch, Grace told them, "I think he overdosed. I think you two don't want to accept it."

Oscar and Juanita looked at her. They didn't know how to respond.

"But if you all are determined to go on with this you might want to speak with Tommy's dad."

"Why would that be?" Juanita asked.

"Right before we broke up, I had a weird talk with Tommy. He'd gotten back from Como, visiting his dad, and I asked him why he'd gone down there. He told me he gave his dad something for safekeeping. I asked him what and he said it was something it was best for me not to know about." She made a grimace. "Tommy could be sort of nasty, couldn't he? The way he was always trying to act like his life was more interesting than your own?"

Oscar nodded. "He sure could be. I wish he was still around though."

"Yeah, I do too. At the same time I'm not going to give him a halo simply because he's no longer with us."

Seven

That night Oscar and Juanita had dinner with Frank at Anderton's, a seafood restaurant on Madison Avenue. They'd ordered a platter of oysters and a pitcher of beer. Frank wore a charcoal gray suit and scarlet tie. Even when he dined at casual places like Anderton's he wore a suit and tie. Juanita was saying, "Oscar thinks Tommy's death sounds suspicious."

"You do?" He shook Tabasco sauce on to an oyster.

"He thinks Tommy might've been involved with some drugs dealers and that might've been why he left Memphis."

"Not that I think he was killed outright or anything," Oscar said, not wanting Frank to think he was paranoid. "I just think he was mixing with a bad crowd his last few months and that might've set off a domino effect. Like maybe the pressure of him hanging out with those people made him shoot up even more than usual." He didn't entirely believe what he was saying. He felt like someone did have a fairly direct hand in Tommy's death. But he didn't want to alarm Frank or have it seem he was chasing after meaningless conspiracies.

Frank swallowed down the oyster and drank from his beer. "I wouldn't be the least bit surprised if he was in some sort of real trouble."

"Really?" asked Oscar.

"You know, it's getting harder not to run with a bad crowd these days. It's like the spine of the country got broken and

we're all running around trying to find our little cubbyholes before the whole goddamn thing stops breathing." He took another sip of his beer. "Everyone has a gun these days. Everyone is aiming at each other."

Oscar said, "This coming from a guy who owns upwards of twenty pistols and revolvers."

"If you took away what a gun is designed for it would be difficult not to see it as having a sleek, stark beauty in its own right."

During parties at his house Frank would sometimes bring a few of his guns downstairs and show them to his friends. They were kept in small wooden boxes stuffed with straw or shredded newspapers. He'd talk about their capabilities and whom he'd bought them from. Mostly he seemed to purchase them from a biker in New Orleans who sold weaponry illegally. Frank claimed the guy even had tommy guns from the thirties and a revolver that had been owned briefly by Bonnie and Clyde. Oscar asked his uncle, "You know much about that city council dude who shot himself back in December? Edward Parker?"

"I don't follow politics. You know that. I never voted in an election in my life."

Juanita poured more beer into her mug. "Yes, Dad, we know you're very proud of your political apathy. But I have this memory of you once saying you knew him at Ole Miss."

"I did know him, though he was several years ahead of me. I never knew him well though. He played football but he wasn't one of the better players. His great grandmother and your grandmother were acquaintances, so when I moved to Oxford, we introduced ourselves to each other. That first year, when I was a freshman, he'd invite me to some of the parties. I never liked them. They were parties where the sons and daughters of the wealthier Delta families drank themselves into a stupor."

"You're one of those sons too," said Juanita.

"I never felt like it. And like doesn't always cling to like."

"You don't know anything else about him?" Oscar asked.

Frank took a camera from the leather satchel setting beside him: it was a Polaroid and not one of his expensive ones. "There was a minor scandal involving him. Nothing major. The rumor was that he had a black girlfriend in town. That in itself would not be so unusual. Lots of Delta princes went around with black women at times, though never anywhere public. But the rumor was that he was practically living with her, that he'd fallen in love with her. Eventually his friends harassed him to the extent where he broke the affair off. There was also a rumor he got her pregnant and that he took her to an abortionist in Baton Rouge to deal with the situation. Again, these are rumors. I can't vouch for them."

Frank raised the camera and took a picture of the massive bar in the center of the room with an elaborate wood chandelier hanging above it. "That was the reason I wanted to come here," he said, lowering the camera and taking out the picture that shot out of its mouth. "We can go whenever ya'll want now."

After leaving Anderton's, Oscar drove downtown and road along the river. He thought about Tommy. He thought about what Grace had said. He parked on the cobblestones that led down to the water and sat on the hood and smoked a joint.

There are no accidents, Tommy had told him over the phone.

He threw the last of the joint on to the cobblestones and watched it roll down toward the water. He had another thought, this time about Juanita. Why was she so invested in helping him? She had not been that close to Tommy. They all ran in the same circle of friends and acquaintances but that circle was large, and though he had seen the two talk together at parties and bars it was never more than for a few minutes.

Around eleven he drove to Maria's apartment building on Rozelle Street, near Immaculate Conception church. He walked up the wooden steps with their flaking white paint and knocked on her door. She opened the door wearing a flannel shirt and pair of shorts. They sat on her couch and snorted a few lines of coke on the mirror on the coffee table and she sat back with her legs tucked under her and looked at him. "How was dinner with your uncle?" she asked.

"Fine. He took a picture of the bar there."

"I've seen some of his pictures. I can't believe they love him in New York like they do."

"Not everybody in New York loves him. Some critics hate him quite a bit. They think he's destroying the art form."

"What do you think?"

"In general I'm in favor of destroying art forms."

Maria laughed. "That really comes across in the music you make these days. It's like you really have it in for melody."

"Melody and me don't get along anymore." He rubbed his nose with the back of his hand, blinking rapidly and glancing over at her. "Though she has been good to me in the past."

"She was that. Back in the day when I used to sit in my bedroom and listen to the Toy Soldiers it was like I would completely drift away for a while. It was like I escaped time and space and found a different way of being in the world. Of course, I would be on acid when I was listening."

"I'm sure that made us sound so much better."

Maria opened a bottle of wine. They drank from it in coffee mugs. She put on Bob Dylan's Blood on the Tracks and they had sex on the low pink couch. Then they sat in the dark huddled together on the couch, watching the calico curtain over the window billow out with the breeze. Maria told him, "You haven't been around much lately."

"I've had a lot on my mind."

"Tommy?"

He nodded, though since it was dark he wasn't sure if she saw him nod. There was an afghan at their feet and he took it and brought it around them. Her apartment always seemed chilly though she had no air-conditioner and the ceiling fans were never on. He said, "Let's go get a drink. The coke made me want to go out and get really drunk."

"One thing leading irreversibly to the other."

"Should we?"

"No. I wish I could but I can't. Actually, I have a paper I need to finish for tomorrow. I should probably get back on it. The professor is a real son of a bitch. He's going to be coming in to class tomorrow just hoping some of us don't have it."

"What's it about?"

"Ophelia."

"What's there to say? Hamlet treated her like shit and she went crazy and drowned herself."

"So you've read Hamlet?"

"Why do you always assume I'm some rock and roll caveman?"

She ran her nails along his thigh. "I guess that's the way I like to think of you."

"I don't think any of my friends have ever met you. They're going to start thinking you're a ghost. Or that I'm making you up."

Oscar went out drinking alone in Overton Square. He found Brian and a few friends at a table in the back of Friday's. He returned to his apartment at seven in the morning. He called Juanita. Surprisingly, she answered on the second ring. He asked, "Why are you helping me out with this? You barely knew the guy."

"Good morning to you too, asshole."

"Good morning, Juanita." He took orange juice out from his refrigerator. "You know, all night long I was wondering. Why? Why are you helping me?"

Juanita clicked her tongue against the roof of her mouth. "We were closer than you thought."

"You dated?"

"No. I wasn't his type and he wasn't mine. He was too earnest for me and I think I wasn't enough of a party girl for him."

"Then how were you close?"

"This can't wait?"

"I'm curious."

"You remember back five or six years ago, when I was engaged to that painter in New York for a few weeks?"

"Yeah, of course I remember. The dude who went up to the Bronx and walked up one of the abandoned buildings there and got on the roof and jumped. I remember." He did remember but it was hazy. He had been busy at that time working on the third and final album by Cosmic. Tommy had left the group by then, not caring for the direction the band was headed, drifting, as it was, toward the sensibility of Lou Reed and Iggy Pop. Tommy loved the Beatles, the Beach Boys. Those were his heroes. But Oscar and their drummer, Stewart Hedges, were pulling away from those sunnier sounds. Noise, echo, and undecipherable lyrics: that was the last incarnation of Cosmic Dust. "How was Tommy involved with what happened?" Oscar asked.

"As you might remember, I was a wreck. I was in love with a guy who'd thrown himself from an abandoned building. Even Dad didn't know what to do with me. He'd come by my place and sit with me and we'd drink and he'd have no idea what to say. But Tommy for some reason did. I ran into him at a diner one night and we started talking. He told me about how he'd felt like throwing himself from some rooftop sometimes and he said that whatever my fiancée did it had nothing to do with me. And the next few weeks, we kept talking. And he kept saying it over and over, how there was nothing I could've done, that some people are just lost to the world and you can't bring them back. He helped me more than anybody else back then."

"I never knew this."

"You were too busy in the studio. And too busy getting high. You were worse than Tommy was, back then."

"I guess I was."

"Anyway, talking to Tommy helped me land on my feet again. It was like he had this terrible grief inside him too, so he could relate to me at that moment. It was like we had the same thing inside of us."

"But it didn't last. It's not like you two became buddies."

"When I got better we didn't have that intense sadness in common anymore. I was down in a pit and he could visit me in that pit because he was down there too. But as soon as I wasn't in that pit, we didn't have much to discuss."

"So you dropped him?"

"Fuck you, Oscar. Why do you always assume the worst about people? I didn't drop him. We just didn't have as much to talk about. The intensity was gone."

Oscar opened his freezer, took out a bottle of vodka. "People who like Cosmic Dust, they always assume I'm the tormented, melancholy guy and Tommy was the happier one. I was Lennon and he was McCartney. But he was always more twisted up than me. He just didn't write songs about it."

"And you, having the luxury of being an asshole, could write all that dark stuff and not think a thing about it."

"That would be one way to put it. Yeah."

After they hung up, Oscar fixed a screwdriver and went out to his apartment door and sat in the canvas chair next to the door. He watched the traffic on Parkway float by in the glimmering morning light. He tried to concentrate on Maria. He tried to focus on what they had done last night. It didn't last. Tommy kept returning, kept moving toward the forefront of his thoughts. Sucking on an ice cube, he went back inside and phoned Information. Then he called the number in Como, Mississippi, and within seconds he was speaking with Tommy's father. "I was wondering if I could drive down and see you about something?" he asked.

Eight

She shopped at night. She did most things at night. She slept in the day and she shopped at night. She went to the Big Star on the corner of Summer Avenue and Highland and loaded the cart with bananas and Pop Tarts, Twinkies and milk. She liked how stores looked late at night: the harsh fluorescent glow, the black windows along the front. Liz wheeled her cart into the bread aisle when she saw him at the end of the aisle. His last name she could not recollect but his first name had been Harry. It had been three years since she'd seen him last. She had pulled his left arm behind his back until it'd popped from its socket.

His back was to her. He slid a bag of Wonder Bread from the shelf and tossed it into his cart. Whistling in the almost silent store, he left the aisle, appearing to be headed for the registers.

No knife and no gun. She had nothing on her. She had both a knife and a gun outside, in her van, but nothing in her jacket and no blade sheathed in her boot. It was time to get better at this. She had been working with Horace for almost a decade. There were individuals who had terrible memories of her. If she tried to count them out, she got to about three dozen. Three dozen individuals in a city the size of Memphis: yeah, the odds were you would have these sudden run-ins.

She stood in the aisle and listened and she heard his voice near the front as he flirted with the young blonde girl at the register. She listened and heard him say goodnight and heard the woman say goodnight. She counted to sixty. Then she pushed her cart, she continued with her shopping.

When she walked outside she saw the spray paint on the side of her van. The letters were black and big and said FUCK YOU BIG FAT CUNT DYKE. She walked to the back door of the van and unlocked it and began loading the grocery bags into the vehicle. There was a knife in a leather sheath she kept in the back of the van. She slid it into the inner pocket of her jacket. Behind her came a whistling noise. She turned with the blade already out from the sheath and lunged at the figure standing a few feet away. She jabbed him in the arm, not bothering to look at his face.

Harry gasped and took many steps back and stared at her with damp eyes. In his hand was a chain: he'd wrapped it around his knuckles. Though his mouth was moving he couldn't get any words out, only air.

Liz glanced at the Big Star. The girl at the register was checking out an older man and they were talking and not looking out the window. No one but her and Harry stood in the parking lot though there were a few cars in the lot around them. She went up to Harry with the knife and marked his cheek. She kicked him in the stomach and once he was on the ground she kicked him in the balls. "You're paying for what you did to my van, you fucking piece of shit," she said. "It's coming out of your fucking wallet."

"The hell I am," he told her. "I'm not paying for shit, you fat bitch."

She lifted her boot, kicking him in the middle of the face. Blood dripped from his mouth and nose. "I'm not paying for shit," he repeated, his voice hoarse, the syllables thick in his throat.

She kicked him again in the head. She kicked him as hard as she had the first time. Maybe harder. The man who had been checking out walked into the lot, wheeling his cart. He looked over and saw them. He stopped and said, "Oh my Lord. Oh Jesus Christ." His hair was white and he appeared to be about sixty but despite his age he was running, he was jogging back into the Big Star. Liz was already in the van. She had started the engine. She glanced out the window at the body on the asphalt. Harry was holding up his arm and pointing his middle finger. His face looked like a ripe tomato that had been squeezed open.

In her apartment she phoned Horace. The groceries were still in their bags on the kitchen table. When he answered, she said, "You ever get tired of this line of work?"

"You having a sudden crisis of conscience?"

"It's not that exactly. It's the inconvenience. I was out shopping just now and ran into Harry something or another, that guy we had to deal with a few years ago."

"I'm no good with last names either."

"He saw me shopping in the store. I didn't think he did but he must have. When I came out he'd sprayed all this shit on the van calling me a dyke and a cunt and shit like that. I had to drive home with that shit right on the side. And it's sitting out in the parking lot now, for all my neighbors to see in the morning."

"He didn't go after you, did he?"

"Yeah, with a chain wrapped around his fist. Never got a chance to touch me with it though. Lucky for me he's no smarter now than he was back then."

"How much did he owe Vince and his guys?"

"Two thousand. I can't remember his name but I can remember that."

"Numbers are more important than names anyway."

She felt better after talking with Horace. Sometimes Horace was all right. There were prints of blood on the orange linoleum floor. She swore to herself and removed her boots and threw them in the bathtub and sprayed them with the shower hose. She put the groceries away and then went through her bedroom closet and found the spray paint near the back, under old shoeboxes. In the parking lot of her apartment building, she shook the can, held it up. She painted both sides with big black circles. Harry had only sprayed one side but she did the other side for the symmetry. In her head she kept thinking about a song Cosmic Dust did on their last album, the title track, a number called "Big Black Chevelle." She once asked Tommy what he thought about the song. She knew the group had recorded it a year or two after he left. "That crap?" he had told her. "That's Oscar all over. It's not him being deep. It's him tricking his fans into thinking he's deep."

The next afternoon she stood in her leopard print T-shirt and underwear in front of the mirror mounted on the closet door of her bedroom and pumped a thirty pound hand barbell, doing ten with the left arm and then ten with the right. There was a hard knock on her door. She dressed in her black jeans and tucked a gun into the back waistband and peered out the curtain. It was Walter, Max's stepbrother. She let him in and he wordlessly sat on the sofa, rubbing his face with his hands. He smelled of alcohol and cigarettes. His balding scalp was pink and the hair along the back of his head hung limply past his neck. "You must realize why I'm here," he finally said as he lowered his hands from his face. "There's only one thing that would send me knocking on your door."

"I don't know where he is."

"You do."

"I don't. And if you don't mind I'd like to get back to my exercises." She gestured toward the door she had closed only a minute before.

"You can't get rid of me that easily."

Liz placed a hand behind her back, touching the gun with her hand but refraining from taking it out. "I bet I can."

"You think I'm weak because I'm not like Max. You think just because I didn't start working for you and Horace after you did what you did to us I'm spineless. But it's not that. It was never that. I was sick of that life. I'd been living that life since I was twelve years old and selling stolen cigarette packs for a cousin of mine. I was sick of it. It wasn't fear. It was just a feeling that I didn't want to wade in shit my whole life."

"I don't really care why you didn't work for us like Max. I don't lay awake at nights wondering."

"I haven't heard from him in a week. Last time I heard from him was Saturday night. We spoke on the phone and he told me he was going out to Jimmy's for a meeting with you and some guys from New Orleans. Some big wigs from down there."

"Max doesn't really know the meaning of discretion, doe he? Shit. Did he ever give you his bank account number too? Or the names and addresses of certain guys he had to rough up over the years?"

"We were family. You tell family things."

"Yeah, some things. And some things you need to hold back for the sake of your family."

"Fuck you, Liz. Tell me what's going on."

"I'm in the same boat as you, Walter. I've been looking for him too."

"His truck, it ain't in front of his house."

"Maybe he ran away."

"And have you guys down his neck for pulling up stakes and leaving? You can't do that shit in your line of business."

"Walter, I'm done. I need to finish my exercise routine."

Walter bolted up from the couch and kicked over the coffee table and said, "Well, I'm not fucking done!"

Liz brought the gun out from the waistband, aiming it at his chest. "That's enough. If I wasn't so concerned about what the neighbors might think I'd shoot you in the goddamn heart right now."

Silence seeped into the room from the ceiling and the walls and the two of them stood in that silence for a few moments. Walter raised his hands and she could see the scars on his palms, scars she'd placed there herself many years ago. He lowered his hands, gripped the edge of the coffee table and placed it back on its legs.

Nine

Oscar got off work at four. He hung up his apron and took off in his Chevelle and picked up Juanita at her apartment. They drove south down I-55 and soon were passing over the border into Mississippi. To their right was a valley with a cluster of tress completely covered in kudzu ivy. The air smelled wet and muddy.

Juanita lowered the volume of the radio. "So what's the story? I can't imagine you told him we're investigating his son's death because we find the circumstances of it suspicious."

Oscar shook his head. "The excuse became overly complicated. I made it up as I was talking to him."

"God forbid you actually develop a plan for this stuff."

"I told him me and a bunch of Tommy's friends were going try to put together an album of material Tommy recorded but never released. I said we were the ones who would be writing the liner notes, you and me, and that we wanted to talk to him to see what Tommy had been up to the last months of his life. I said I'd lost touch with him."

"I guess that last part is true."

"And he did record a lot of solo material over the years."

"You and your buddies plan to release any of it?"

He nodded no. He said, "I can imagine Brian taking up a project like that at some point but nobody has anything in the works now."

There was a farmhouse standing in a field in the distance

with Christmas lights dripping from its eaves and a horse trotting near its porch and they drove up around a bend and it vanished behind branches. They drove further south.

Some nights while traveling through the country on the tour bus Tommy would talk about his dad. Tommy's father had grown up in Como, where his father and grandfather had been lawyers, and where his great-grandfather had owned a grocery store before getting killed during the battle at Antietam. Tommy's father didn't want to become a lawyer and didn't think he had the temperament needed to address judges and juries and frame together arguments. He became a dentist instead. He opened a practice in Memphis so as not to compete with the main dentist in Como, whose wife was a friend of his mother's. Once in Memphis, he met and married the daughter of a journalist at The Commercial Appeal. Tommy was born a year later. The marriage lasted for almost twenty years. But then it fell apart rapidly and drunkenly and his father returned to Como, living alone in the family house.

Soon they were driving up to that house, a two-story Victorian with a turret on one side and a steeply pitched gable on the other. Weeping willows stood in the yard and partially masked the front of the structure.

"How are ya'll doing this evening?" Tommy's father said as he shook their hands on the porch. He was a stout man, with feathery white hair and a creased face. His shake was very firm, as Tommy's had always been. That was always a surprise about Tommy, how he looked delicate and withdrawn but his handshake was firm.

"Thanks for having us over," Oscar said. "That couldn't be nicer of you." He held up a bottle of whiskey. "For your hospitality." Then he introduced Tommy's father to Juanita.

"Call me Jack," he said.

"Good to meet you, Jack." She smiled, shaking his hand. Jack led them through the front door, around the staircase in the middle of the house, and back into the kitchen, where he had gumbo simmering.

For the first hour they ate and drank the whiskey. Dean Martin crooned from the stereo in the den. Jack said his mother had grown up in New Orleans before moving to Como and the recipe he used had been hers. He still had a notebook she had compiled of her own recipes. He never cooked until the divorce, he explained, but after he moved here he realized he would have to learn how to do so. "I could've hired one of the colored ladies in town, I imagine," he said, "but it's not like how it used to be." He shook Tabasco sauce over his bowl. "If you hire a colored woman these days you don't know what thoughts might be running through her head. They might smile and be pleasant but they might secretly hate your guts. I don't want someone who hates my guts cooking and cleaning for me. No way. The colored, most of them are good people, but after they let all those hell-raisers take over, I don't know, it's like they think every single white person was put on this earth just to torment them."

Oscar glanced across the table and saw Juanita about to respond. And he could imagine that response. When Martin Luther King had been assassinated in Memphis, she had gone around saying whites deserved all the rioting that took place, and a lot more than that too. She'd been fourteen at the time and had gotten into a few fights at her school because of her opinions. Oscar stared across the kitchen table and raised an eyebrow that implied: If you get into some argument with this guy we're never going to get what we came here for. She looked back. Her look said: Okay, but I don't like this.

Oscar changed the subject. "After you moved back here, did Tommy visit often?" He shook more filè powder over his gumbo and took another corncob from the platter dish in the center of the table.

"He did. A lot of my friends, they do all these things with their sons. Hunting, fishing, things like that. We went fishing when he was younger but he never liked it much, said it bored him. And I was never one for hunting myself. I think deer and ducks are beautiful. I don't see why anyone would ever set out to harm one. So we never did that either. We never had those things to bond over. With Tommy, even early on it was always music, music, music. Elvis and the Beatles and those Rolling Stone guys, he loved them. Some of the colored guys too. Ray Charles, and that guy with the big hair who always looks a little queer."

Juanita looked up. "Little Richard?"

"That sounds right. Him. My point is, despite how little we had in common, we did like to spend time together." He took off his glasses, rubbed his eyes. He placed his glasses back on.

By ten they were in the living room drinking more of the whiskey. Glenn Miller and his band drifted from the console. Oscar and Juanita were on the leather couch. Jack sat in an orange upholstered chair with low arms and a high back. "I know you didn't come all the way down here to hang out with an old man like myself." He grinned, the creases on his face deepening. "So what kind of things did you want to know about Tommy for this record you're putting together?"

Juanita leaned forward, her glass in her hand. "In Memphis some of Tommy's friends had the impression he was maybe depressed or anxious about something these last few months. You know of any reason why that might be true? Why he might've been depressed or anxious?"

"Well, the drugs. That was a terrible thing. A terrible, terrible thing."

Oscar asked, "You mean him getting so addicted to them?"

"Yeah, exactly. What else would I be talking about? He started smoking pot back in high school. I knew it too. I could smell it. When I was young, really young, I used to go to these rowdy poker games. I didn't do it often. It never was my scene. But some of the guys there would smoke that crap." He looked at Juanita. "Excuse my language. But they would. Pot wasn't invented in the fifties. People think it was but it wasn't. It wasn't around near as much but it was there and I knew the smell of it from those parties." He scratched the tip of his nose, sunk deeper into his chair.

Juanita sipped from her drink and placed it on the coaster. "You and Tommy get into fights about it?"

"All the time. I'd yell at him, I'd tell him how bad it was, how it was hard to get off the stuff once you started." He stared down at his glass and crossed his legs. "He never listened. It got worse and worse."

"Was there anything more than the drugs making him uneasy?" Oscar asked. "He seemed to be hanging out with a rougher crowd than usual the last few months before he left Memphis."

Jack stared at him hard through his glasses. "These are some mighty peculiar questions if all you're going to do is write a tribute to him on the back of an album. What exactly are you trying to dredge up here about my son? I don't quite get it."

Oscar poured more whiskey over the ice in his glass. "I'm sorry, Jack. I don't mean any offense. Part of this is personal, to be straight up honest with you. Tommy and me, we used to be close. Part of me simply wants to know what was going on with him this last year or so. I don't know why exactly. I think it's because I feel guilty about not being closer to him during a time when he could've used his friends."

Jack adjusted his glasses. He swiveled the ice in his glass. He didn't say anything.

Juanita took over. "Tommy's death shook many people up. It was clear he was taking too many drugs. Everybody knew that. But what isn't clear is why he left for Arizona. It's also not clear why he was acting so anxious the last few months. So we're trying to get a full picture. We want it so we can do right by him when we talk about his life in the liner notes. But we always want that full picture for ourselves. So there's a purely selfish motive going on too. I won't lie about that."

Jack reached over to the coffee table and grabbed the bottle of whiskey and slowly unscrewed the top and poured more into his glass. He screwed the top back on. He said, "If I told the two of you something strange that was going on with him, would it stay here, just between the three of us?" He leaned back, drank from the whiskey.

"It would," said Juanita.

Oscar nodded.

"I don't want this appearing in no liner notes."

"It won't," Oscar assured him.

"All right. This stays between us, now. One of his last trips down here, we were playing chess out in the backyard. It was early February but it was a freakishly warm, so we were playing in the sun in the backyard, getting some fresh air. We were just chatting. I could tell he was a little high but as long as he never did drugs in my house, and I don't think he ever did, I didn't complain. I should've but I'd given up on that front. I prayed for him all the time but I knew me complaining to him wouldn't make any difference." Jack grew still. He inhaled and exhaled and looked at the wallpaper across the room. Finally, he said, "Tommy told me he was hanging out with some pretty tough customers these days. He said Memphis was getting rougher and he'd fallen in with some real tough guys. He said they were fun to hang around but he'd started getting scared of them."

"What were they up to?" Juanita asked. "Why was he getting scared?"

"He assured me he wasn't in danger, nothing like that. He just said it was getting to the point where he started to know things he didn't want to know. Well, I got alarmed at that, right away. I said, 'Tommy, what the hell are you talking about? You need to go to the police with something?' He didn't like how I was acting. I could see it on his face. I used to have this uncle. He was a gambler and he sold gin all along the Gulf Coast back in the Prohibition days. I used to tell Tommy stories about him when Tommy was a kid the way some parents might tell pirate stories, ghost stories. I reckon Tommy thought I'd find the notion of him hanging out with dangerous people exciting, just like I used to find

65

the stories about my uncle exciting. But it's two entirely different things, you know. What's okay for a long dead uncle isn't okay with a son."

"So he didn't get anymore specific?" Oscar asked.

"He tried to play it all down. He said he didn't really hang out with these people, he only knew them from bars, local folklore, that sort of thing. He gave me an example. He said there was a woman named Liz. She was one of these toughs around town. She dressed up like some guy from a motorcycle gang: leather jacket, leather pants. He said she worked as the muscle for certain not particularly pleasant individuals."

"He give a last name?" Juanita asked.

"No last names. He mentioned this other person too. This guy named Richard. He said he was this super thin guy. And he was Liz's boyfriend. Or kind of a boyfriend. He said it was funny seeing the two of them out because Liz was so fat and this guy was so thin. Tommy also said they'd get into fights and Liz would get up and act like she was going to punch him and this guy would pretend to cower and then they'd both start to laugh like it was all okay."

"You seem to remember this conversation really well," commented Juanita. She took a cigarette from her purse.

"It was the last actual talk I had with him. Of course I remember it well. He did visit one more time. But he wasn't, shall we say, communicative. He was clammed up. I think the drugs were getting bad by then. I pleaded with him and told him he had to quit, told him the drugs were killing him. That was when he told me he was moving to Tucson. I asked him why he was going and he told me he needed the change. That was as much of an answer as I ever got."

Oscar asked, "What did you think about it? Him leaving, I mean."

Jack shrugged. "I thought it might do him good. I thought Memphis was bringing him down. I thought he had a lot of friends who were into drugs and maybe getting away from them would help out. He didn't tell me that was why he was going but that was what I surmised."

Oscar thought about a Richard he knew. This Richard was skinny and eerily pale and Oscar had last seen him at the Sex Pistols concert in the Taliesyn Ballroom back at the turn of the year, when the group was playing their second concert in the States. Richard played drums with a few local acts, mainly groups inspired by that Sex Pistols concert, and Oscar had heard from Brian that Richard played with Tommy at one of Tommy's studio sessions, though eventually Tommy got rid of him because of his lack of drumming skills.

"Thanks for talking to us," Oscar told Jack.

Shortly after midnight Jack took them upstairs to the guest rooms. He showed Juanita her room first and then led Oscar into the second room in the hallway. He told Oscar the room had been Tommy's and that Tommy had left some journals in there and Oscar was free to take any if he wished. "I looked through them, I don't know why," he said. "I looked through them the night I heard he was gone. I thought about throwing them away without looking at them. I thought reading them might be an invasion of his privacy. But curiosity got the better of me."

"You sure it's okay if I look through them too?"

"Yeah. There's some poems in them, some song lyrics. That's why I brought it up. Since you two used to be partners that way, I thought you might find it interesting, seeing what he was up to."

Oscar said goodnight to Jack, unzipped his bag and changed into his pajamas and robe. As he dressed, he looked up at the posters on the wall of Janis Joplin and Pink Floyd and Sly Stone and David Bowie. The closet still had some of Tommy's clothes, mainly shirts and a few jeans folded on a shelf, but there was also a black suit near the back, hanging behind the other clothes. Oscar searched through the pockets of the shirts and jeans. He found sticks of gum and a few movie tickets and receipts from Big Star and Kroger's. He found a guitar pick that he placed in the pocket of his robe.

The last item he searched was the suit. In the breast pocket of the suit coat was a piece of paper with a phone number. It had a Memphis area code. Oscar placed that in the pocket of his robe too.

He stepped over to the journals setting on the desk across from the bed. There were three of them: spirals notebooks with the month and year written on the cover. The first read January 78. The second said December 76. The third, November 74.

He brought them over to the bed. He lit a cigarette and sat down on the pillows, his back against the headboard. Many of the pages were filled lyrics or random thoughts or quotations from John Lennon and Jack Kerouac and St. Teresa. Other pages were pencil drawings of faces. There were faces of some of Tommy's ex-girlfriends and also the faces of all of the members of Cosmic Dust. Oscar looked closely at his own, which he found in the journal marked November 74. It showed him with the type of hair he had back then, long and hanging in thick curls on his shoulders. In the drawing he also had the beard he'd grown in the early seventies. He looked like a burnt out hippie or a jaded beach bum.

Near the back of the same journal he came upon a poem fragment, or set of unfinished lyrics, that he read several times.

Maria, Maria, with the dark long tresses
Maria, my Maria, nearing the hours of your muddy white dress
Maria with your eyes and symphonic rainy clatter
Your mammalian hair and brow
We were twelve by the pond
I waited near the pond
For you
Maria.

It was nearing four by the time he switched off the lamp.

Ten

He drove around the roads in Overton Park for ten minutes before he found Richard stepping out from a bright red Impala SS and waving at the driver of the car and watching the car speed off under the tunnel of branches. Oscar watched him from his black Chevelle as he crept up. Richard took a white envelope from the pocket of his jeans, smiled at it, and placed it back in the pocket. As the Chevelle grew nearer Richard glanced up. He saw Oscar at the steering wheel. He came over, leaning his head into the open passenger window. "What are you doing here, man?" he asked.

"I have some questions about Tommy."

"What kind of questions?"

"About why he left for Tucson. About how he died."

"He died because he was a junkie. He died the same way I'll probably die." He stepped away from the car. "Go on, man. I don't have anything to say. I'm busy."

"Busy doing what?"

"Fuck you. You know exactly what I'm busy doing."

Richard started walking away. Oscar took the keys from the ignition and bolted from the Chevelle and ran up to Richard, pulling at his arm. "This is serious fucking shit," he said. "I'm not joking around here."

"Leave me alone." Richard yanked his arm away and Oscar grabbed it again and Richard swung his fist into Oscar's face and Oscar fell to his knees, grunting. Then Oscar was up again and grabbing on to Richard's shoulders and elbows and Richard brought his head around in a smooth arc and rammed it into Oscar's head, sending them both to the ground. Oscar could taste blood on the tip of his tongue. He crawled across the grass over to Richard and Richard rose up and threw a fist toward his chin but this time he ducked and the hand and arm flew past his shoulder. Oscar lunged into Richard's torso. Now they were rolling around and grunting and Richard had his hand on Oscar's face, pulling hard at his nose and mouth, and Oscar had his hand in Richard's long spiky hair, winding it up into his fingers. Then he pulled at the hair with his entire body.

Richard screamed. He yelled out, "Fuck, fuck, fuck!" Richard elbowed him in the face and then in the throat. Oscar fell back into the grass and looked up at the gray sky, his skull feeling as if it had been removed from his neck and thrown against a concrete wall and then placed back on his neck. When he opened his mouth blood spilled out from under his tongue. The inside of his cheek burned with pain.

He heard Richard stand up and curse and tell him to stand up too. Oscar turned over on to his stomach, managed to rise up on his hands and knees. Richard was looking out at the park road and saw a pick-up truck idling with a shirtless guy in overalls staring at them from the driver's window. The guy yelled through his open window, "You two girls look like you're having a real party out there."

"We're okay," Richard told him.

"You ain't going to kill each other, are you?"

Richard shook his head. "We're fine. Just playing around."

"I might not mind getting into some of that action," he said. "I like kicking the shit out of fags almost as much as I like making them suck my dick." He laughed and rolled back up his window. The truck drove off. Richard said, "That could've been the fucking pigs, man. You could've gotten me in trouble."

"You think he might call the police?" Oscar was standing now, wiping the blood off his mouth and nose with the backs of his hands.

"No way, man. I know that guy. I've never been with him but I've heard tales from some of the guys around here. He's this real sick redneck. Sick in his mind and sick in his soul." He took some tissues from his pocket and held them to the back of his scalp.

Oscar looked at the blood on his hands. "You messed me up. Shit. This is a new shirt too."

"You were the one starting shit."

"You were the one to ratchet it up way beyond where it needed to go."

"I don't like having my arm pulled and I don't have a thing to say about Tommy."

"Can't you just talk for a minute?"

"Tommy's dead. Let the guy rest."

"How much you get paid for, say, ten minutes?"

"That's not how the pay scale tends to be arranged."

"I'll pay you seventy bucks."

"Really? Just to answer some questions about Tommy?"

"Sound fair?"

"Yeah. Whatever you want to know about Tommy, I'm pretty sure I won't know it. But for seventy bucks, I'll tell you what I do know."

They started walking to his car. Oscar admitted, "I don't have the money right now, though. I'll get it tonight and can pay you tomorrow."

Richard stopped in his steps. "Hell no. You pay me now."

Oscar sighed. He wiped more blood off his lips with the palm of is hand. "You are really a frustrating individual."

"You put seventy dollars in my hand and I'll talk. I'll answer to the best of my ability. I won't be saying a word until then."

Oscar knew he could probably get the money from Frank that very day as long as Frank was home. And he only lived five minutes away, across from Overton Park. "Okay, give me your address," he said. "We'll meet at your place tonight."

After he left the park he drove down to Frank's house and saw Frank's Buick in the carport. As he got out of his car he heard music drifting from the open windows of the house, the sound of Frank playing on the piano in the den. He knocked on the door. The piano stopped and Frank appeared at the door and looked him over. "You look bad, son," he told Oscar. "You need to start taking better care of yourself."

Oscar cleaned up in the bathroom. He washed his face and held a washrag to his lip until the bleeding stopped and took some band-aids from the medicine cabinet and placed them on the cuts along his brow. He found Frank at the piano again. He was playing as if he had forgotten he'd just let Oscar into the house. He hummed along as he played. But as Oscar walked up to him, Frank spoke. "You feeling better?" he asked.

"At least I feel cleaner."

They went out to the screen porch. Frank turned on the ceiling fan and sat on the wicker lounge seat, putting his feet up. They both lit cigarettes. Oscar didn't sit down. He needed to pace. The fight had stirred him up. "You aren't exactly the fighting type, Oscar," Frank said. "I'd be curious to hear what happened."

The night after they ate at Anderton's, Juanita had told Oscar she thought it would be better to keep her father in the dark about Tommy. She said the more she thought about it the more likely it seemed Frank would tell her to stop asking questions regarding him. Frank worried about her, she said. As nonchalant as he appeared in most areas of his life he would not be nonchalant about her becoming entangled in a murder mystery. Oscar turned to Frank. He said, "I got into a fight with a friend of mine. It was stupid. We were arguing over money."

"He owes you or you him?"

"I owe him. He's been getting me this special weed and I've been buying it on credit. The diner where I work, it doesn't pay much."

"How much you owe?"

"Close to seventy dollars."

"Oscar, how much weed have you been smoking? Hell."

"It's good stuff. Plus this has been over a period of time."

"That's something I've never understood. You made all that money when you were singing back in the sixties? What did you do with it? You bury it in somebody's yard? Spend it all on wine, women, and song?"

"The record company got a big chunk. So did our manager. And the rest, yeah, I burned through it. That car out there is the last evidence I have that I was ever a semiwealthy man."

"You ever tempted to sing with another successful band?"

"Not really. Not if it means doing things I don't want to do. You ever tempted to take pictures for an advertising agency?"

"All right. I see the point you're trying to make."

Frank went upstairs and Oscar could hear him walking around, rummaging through desk drawers. Soon he brought down some bills. Then they walked out to the cinderblock shed in the backyard, which was where Frank had his studio, and looked over the pictures Frank thought might work well for the solo album Oscar had been working on for several months. Seven or eight photographs hung from pegs attached to a wire. The one Frank thought might work best was of his black cat Dorothy tongue bathing in Frank's bedroom, with its crimson wallpaper. As usual, none of the images had titles. "I like it too," Oscar said. "It'll make the album seem like music for cats."

"To be listened to in red rooms," added Frank.

Oscar met Juanita for dinner at Buntyn's Café on Southern Avenue. As they drank coffee and ate chicken and dumplings they looked over the lines Oscar had copied from Tommy's journals: the lines that seemed most relevant to their questions. On one page in his journal Tommy had written Liz will kill Richard only if Richard does not kill Liz first. I mean this metaphorically/spiritually. They are both made of ash and bone and will never truly die. They both belong to the realm of red night skies. Another passage, one of the last in the last notebook, stated I am a pawn in a game that has led to a man shooting himself. Will God remember this? Do pawns matter to Him when Bishops, Knights, and Queens plague this world? And yet another said I can bring them down. What's holding me back? I'm like Hamlet (though without the dead Father and the kingdom). God, tell me when to scream.

Juanita sipped from her coffee mug. "You're going look worse tomorrow. All those bruises are just waiting to come out full bloom."

Oscar touched his swollen lip. "I have work tomorrow. Sometimes, I guess, it's good to work in the kitchen, where no one is looking at you. I won't have a thousand customers asking questions."

"I still don't get it. Why did he attack?"

"Have you met this guy?"

"I haven't had the pleasure."

"He's under the impression he's Sid Vicious."

"You know that I think? I think his response had something to do with Tommy." She placed her mug down and lit a cigarette. "I think when you said you wanted to talk about Tommy, a fuse burnt out in his head. He knows shit he doesn't want to know and his first response was to attack. It was feral. It wasn't him just trying to act all punk."

"You might be right. I just wish I was on the receiving end of that fuse blowout." He pointed to her cigarette pack. Juanita nodded, sliding the pack over to him.

Outside the window, a skinny white guy with huge hair walked by. He was shirtless and bare foot and he carried a radio from which Elton John was blasting. Juanita said, "I'm coming with you tonight. You need my help facing this guy."

"No I do not. I don't need your help and you're not coming with me. I don't trust this guy and I don't want you getting mixed up with him."

"I'm coming."

"You most certainly are not."

Eleven

They arrived at his apartment building around nine. He lived close to Frank: only a few blocks south. Frank faced one side of Overton Park and Richard's apartment building another. Richard answered the door in a ratty red bathrobe. His left eye was bruised and his hair was tucked under a white bandanna. Oscar introduced him to Juanita. "You going to be our referee?" he asked, grinning.

"If it comes to that, yeah," she told him."

Richard perched on an orange hassock with straw stuffing sticking out from a rip in its side. Oscar and Juanita sat on two metal folding chairs that surrounded the coffee table. Oscar held up the wad of bills and leaned over the table and counted them out until he reached seventy. Richard chuckled. "Shit, you really did come through, man. I thought you were just talking."

Oscar kept his hand over the bills. "You get this as soon as you answer some questions."

Richard rubbed his nose with the back of his forearm. Snot kept dripping from it toward his lip. "These must be some serious questions."

"They might be," Juanita told him. "That's what we're trying to find out. With your assistance, of course."

"Go ahead. Let them roll." He rubbed his hands together.

Oscar looked over at Juanita. She went first. "Who is Liz?"

Richard flashed her a stony look: it was as if she'd spat out some insult toward him. "Liz?"

"Yeah. Who is Liz?"

"She's this big girl I hang out with. She's fun. She's okay."

"Tommy knew her?" Oscar asked.

He nodded. His eyes were paying close attention to their faces now.

"What kind of relationship did he and Liz have?" Juanita was using a gentle tone. Gentle but urgent.

"How do you even know about her? Tommy talk about her?" He took off his bandana. He rubbed the back of his oily hair.

"Yeah," Oscar lied, trying to keep the dialogue as simple as possible. "He did."

Richard rubbed his nose again. He bounced his knee wildly. "Listen, I think I need to know what these questions are for before I go any further. I get the sense you two are up to something."

"So you don't want the seventy dollars?" Oscar lifted the bills from the table and started rolling them into a wad again.

"I do, man. Of course I do. I just don't like being out of the loop."

"Tell us a little about Liz." Juanita smiled warmly at Richard. "We really aren't asking for very much."

Richard stood up. He peeked out the front curtains. He closed the curtains. "Liz is a woman who has paved her own way through the world. She's big and she can be mean and I suspect she's killed a few people through the years."

"People like Tommy?" Oscar asked.

"Fuck no. She liked Tommy. She liked that group you guys were in, Cosmic Debris or whatever."

"Cosmic Dust," Oscar corrected him.

"Yeah. She liked you guys. When she heard me and Tommy were hanging out and playing together sometimes, she got real excited. I was the one who introduced them. I've known Liz for three years, I guess, and I introduced her to

Tommy about a year ago."

"Her and Tommy hit it off?" Juanita was standing too, moving toward Richard, her hands clasped behind her back.

"They did. Not as much as me and her. We have this special bond based on all sorts of nasty things, shit that would make your toes curl if I told you about it. But they liked each other. The three of us hung out at times. Never in bars, though. Liz isn't into the bar scene. We'd hang out here or at Tommy's place."

Oscar stood now. All three of them were by the window, with its shut calico curtain. "What did they talk about?"

"Tommy was fascinated by her bad-assness. Here was this chick who wore leather and carried brass knuckles and a bunch of knives. He thought it was exciting. That was why I was drawn to her at first too, until things got a lot deeper between us. As for her, she thought Tommy was a genius. His moodiness, to her, was only further proof of it."

Richard returned to the hassock. He rubbed his scalp with both hands and made a groaning noise and glanced up at Oscar and said, "My head still hurts like hell from what you did."

"My face doesn't feel any better."

Juanita and Oscar slowly returned to the folding chairs and sat down. Juanita said, "You think she's killed people?"

He rubbed his nose. He bounced his knee. He murmured, "I should be keeping my mouth shut. I'm only talking as much as I am because I snorted some coke right before ya'll got here."

Juanita scooted her chair closer to Richard. "Richard, we think Tommy died under suspicious circumstances."

Richard wiped his nose with the back of his hand and snorted. "The pigs think this too, or is this a theory between the two of you?"

"It's between the two of us," Oscar told him, "but it's getting close to being more than a theory."

There was a knock on the door, loud and abrupt. Richard looked at them. "Were you two followed?"

"No," Juanita said. "Not that we would notice it."

"Shit," Richard said. He jogged up to the curtain and glanced out and laughed. "It's the guy next door, that's all. Probably wants to ask for a cup of sugar."

He opened the door and a black man in a camouflage tank top came in. Richard introduced him to Juanita and Oscar. His name was Noah. After they shook hands, Noah said to Richard, "You've the book, right?"

"Sure do. Be right back."

He went into his bedroom and returned with a book wrapped in a black silk cloth. He gave it to Noah and Noah winked at Richard and thanked him. Then he said it was nice meeting Juanita and Oscar and he left. As Richard closed the door, he said, "Among other things, Liz is the purveyor of a certain type of literature."

"Who would've been following us?" asked Juanita. "Liz?"

"Maybe. Her or her people."

Oscar thought about asking for Liz's address or phone number. He wasn't sure, though, if he wanted to go that far yet. It sounded like Liz was not the type of person you simply approached with a list of questions. Instead, he said, "Tommy was bothered by this city council guy who killed himself. A man named Edward Parker. He sent Juanita a clip about him from Tucson. Do you know why Tommy might've had this interest?"

"I don't. I haven't the foggiest."

"You're lying," said Juanita.

"How can you tell?"

"You grimaced as soon as Oscar said the name."

He itched his nose. He looked down at the floor, his hand on his hip. He looked up and said, "I can't say anything about it."

"You sure?" asked Juanita. "The seventy goes with us."

"You two are making me pay for every goddamn dime of it."

Oscar shrugged. "Yes we are."

"I liked Tommy too, all right? And if I thought he'd been killed somehow, I would want that person fried by the state, okay? But I don't buy it. The cops out in Arizona thought it was an overdose and I suspect they know a lot more about this kind of shit than you guys."

Juanita was sitting with her legs crossed. She gazed hard at Richard. "You grimaced at the name. I saw you. Tell us why."

Richard considered this. He placed his bandana back on his head. "Here's what I think. I think it's better not to go around asking questions about certain things. You might not like the answers."

"Tell us about Edward Parker," Oscar said. "Tell us what connection Tommy had with this guy and we'll leave. We'll go with the seventy dollars still on the table."

"All right. Shit." He cracked his knuckles and swiveled his shoulders. "Tommy and Liz were up to something regarding that guy. I'm not lying when I say I don't know exactly what it is. But there were a few times when I would be out of the room and I'd come back in and it'd be clear they were talking about him. Tommy and Liz, they know I have a big mouth. Shit, I have a big mouth right now, telling you guys this. So they wanted to keep it tucked away from me, I guess."

"When you heard stuff, what did you hear?" asked Juanita.

"They had pictures of this Edward Parker in a situation he would not like to be made public. That's all I know. I never saw the pictures and I never asked questions. I live my own life, you know? I have it hard enough without asking questions."

Oscar slid the seventy across the coffee table toward Richard. "Anything else you know that might help us?"

Juanita leaned forward with her hands on her knees, almost as if she were posing for a picture. "Remember, he was your friend too."

"There's a diner on South Parkway, close to downtown, where Liz and Tommy used to get lunch. I went with them once. There's a dude there named Randy, a real tall black guy. He's a manager there I think. The time we got lunch, it was clear he was involved with the pictures somehow."

"How was it clear?" Oscar said.

"I'm a junkie, okay? I was high out of my mind when I was there. I can't offer up details because it was all a fog anyway. But trust me, he was involved. I have an antenna for this kind of thing."

Juanita picked up her snakeskin purse and stood. "The name of the place, what is it?"

"Ella's. It's named after the old lady who owns it."

In the parking lot Oscar said, "It should be pretty clear now, don't you think? Tommy didn't die of any overdose."

"Yeah. I agree. But we still don't have anything to take the cops."

Oscar opened the door of his Chevelle and grabbed a flask from under the driver's seat and drank and handed it to Juanita. She nodded no, she said she was too keyed up to drink. "I'm keyed up too and that's exactly why I'm drinking," Oscar said. He screwed the top back on. "We might be diving into some real shit here. Are we ready for it?"

"We don't have a choice."

"We could stop going around asking questions. That seems like a pretty damn big choice, if you ask me."

"We could. But we're getting too close."

"And if we stop, it's like we let Tommy down."

"There's that to."

Oscar shook his head. "Of all the people he knew why should we be the ones burdened with this?"

"I guess we got lucky."

Part Two: Sound and Vision

April and May 1978

Twelve

Liz saw the door of Richard's place closing as she drove up to the apartment building. So she put the van in reverse and quickly backed out of the apartment building's parking lot and instead parked in the far corner of the empty lot across the street, under some branches. She sat in the dark of her car and waited and watched. After ten minutes passed, the curtains moved: it was Richard peeking out, seeing if she was there. But he would not see her across the street because it wouldn't cross his mind to look. A smarter, more calculating person would. Tommy would. But Richard wasn't that person and Richard was not like Tommy.

She rolled down her window and could smell the sweet, sickly air. A row of Bradford pear trees were in bloom along the edge of the lot, their branches looking as if they were covered by white butterflies. She remembered how she had loved spring as a girl. She remembered walking down to a creek not far from the house where she grew up. She would walk there alone and put her feet in the water and stay there an entire afternoon reading Nancy Drew mysteries. Daylight would shift through the branches overhead. It would be good to be away from people. Even at that age she hated most of them.

The door opened. She squinted. She wished she had her binoculars with her but they were at her apartment. Two figures made their way along the landing and down the steps. In the parking lot they walked close to a streetlight. The woman she did not recognize. She was pretty, with a mass of curly brown hair that fell to her shoulders. But the other person she knew, though she had only seen him in the distance, on a stage, singing. He had band-aids around one eye and his lip seemed to have dried blood on it but she knew him. Part of her had realized there was a chance this would happen. Part of her was excited.

They drove away, going west in the direction of downtown and the river. She considered following them. She decided to deal with Richard instead. She hammered her fist against Richard's door.

When he opened it she grabbed him by the back of his neck and led him into the bedroom and threw him on the bed and spat on him. Richard laughed as she did this. He wiped the spit from his cheek and laughed. She saw the bruises and scrapes on his cheeks. "Why were you talking to those people?" she asked. "Far as I know you aren't friends with that guy."

"Liz, I love it when you're angry and afraid."

"I'm not afraid."

He made a hissing noise with his lips and said, "But you are very, very angry."

"You need to tell me why they were here, you little faggot?"

"I'm not a faggot."

"You don't know what you are."

He took a pack of Newport cigarettes from the bedside table and lit one. "But I do, Liz. A faggot ain't no different from a straight. One likes cock and one likes pussy. They're two sides of one coin. I'm another breed entirely. I like everything. I don't think they have a word for what I am and I don't think they ever will."

She made a face. "Aren't we so dear and original."

"Yes, we are. And you love me for it." He blew smoke in her direction. "Exactly how pissed off are you?"

"You want to find out?"

"Might as well. I don't have any other plans tonight." He

flicked the cigarette at her and it struck her shoulder and fell to the small oval rug at her feet. Liz stared at it and then brought her boot down, crushing it into the fabric of the dirty rug. "I'm going to ask you again what those two wanted. I don't think you realize what you're in for if you don't answer."

"Fuck you."

She grabbed his feet, pulled him towards her. He must've noticed a glint in her eye because he brought his hands up to fend her off. It was too late. She took a rubber ball from her jacket pocket, forced it into his mouth. She took masking tape from the same pocket and taped his lips shut and then taped his flailing arms together at the wrists. He was moaning, making pleading noises with his chest and throat. She brought her hand back and struck him as hard as she could across his cheek. The sound it made was soft and terrible. She struck him again, this time with her other fist. He whimpered. His nose was now crooked and blood poured from it. As he rolled on the mattress away from her she caught him by his hair and pulled him back and pounded him several times in the ribs. His body had turned hard, as if it were a single coiled muscle. Liz grabbed the bed sheet, pressed it to his nostrils. "No more games."

He nodded. Tears dampened his cheeks.

"They were here to ask about Tommy?"

He nodded. He blinked his wet eyes.

"Why?" She removed the making tape as gently as she could from his mouth and he spat the rubber ball out on to the floor.

He gasped and when the gasping settled down, he said, "They think he was killed."

"Why do they think this?"

"I don't know." He had a difficult time forming the words. "They wouldn't tell me."

"You couldn't be bothered to ask?"

"Fuck all of you. I'm just trying to get by. Keep me out of this."

She raised her fist. She brought it down into the center of his stomach. He curled up and pushed his face into the sheet and sobbed. "You're in this even if you don't want to be." She spoke softly. Her legs were weak and she felt nauseous. "Tell me exactly what you told them."

It took a few minutes to coax the information out of him. She didn't hit him anymore, fearing any other strikes might knock him out. After he was done going over the meeting she went into the kitchen and found a pair of scissors in the drawer and brought it into the bedroom. His eyes widened. She shook her head and laughed. She cut off a strip of sheet and held it out to him, saying to hold it to his nose. She was going to drive him to an emergency room.

In the van they didn't say a word. She didn't play the radio. Only as they approached the bright lights of the hospital on Union Avenue did he turn and say, "I think we should take a break from each other."

She brought the van up to the back of Methodist Hospital. "We can do that, though I might be dropping by with more questions. And to check up on how you're doing. Maybe I'll bring some soup. I'll bring a can of Campbell's with me."

Richard took the cloth from his nose, glanced down at the mess of snot and blood on it. His eyes had dried. "You hurt me for real this time. I was going to tell you everything. I was only playing."

"Playtime is over," she told him. She caressed the back of his neck. She said, "Make sure those doctors keep you pretty. I'm going to be real sad if you come out of this place looking any different."

After he walked through the glass doors of the emergency room she drove around downtown Memphis and thought through the situation. She would not tell Horace: not yet. She would keep this to herself. If she told Horace then Horace might tell Vince and that would not be good. She would watch Oscar. She would try to protect him in her fashion.

Thirteen

Oscar and Juanita took the booth near the jukebox. The jukebox itself was unlit and dusty and a broom rested against its side. The space was small but crowded. Most of the customers were black. Two women in purple blouses walked around taking orders. There was a man at the cashier register. He looked like he was in his mid-thirties. He wore a short-sleeve white shirt and a black tie and he had a jagged scar on his left cheek.

Juanita said, "You think that might be him by the register?"

"I'll go check," Oscar said.

He went across the diner, toward the sign that read RESTROOMS hanging over a hallway, and as he passed the man at the register he glanced at the nametag. It said RANDY. Oscar washed his hands in the restroom and returned to the table and nodded yes.

The waitress approached their table. After they ordered, Juanita said, "Now comes the hard part."

"I think we should just mention Tommy. We lie a little. We can say Tommy mentioned him."

"Yeah. Try to gauge his reaction."

As they ate their lunch of patty melts and meat loaf they discussed what they knew. They tried to arrange the pieces. Oscar felt the way he did when writing a new song: especially a song that had pieces that did not seem to be fitting together into a whole.

The waitress came by. They ordered more coffee.

They kept talking. There were the clear aspects of the situation. Tommy had told Oscar his death would not be accidental. Which meant that it would be carried out on purpose. Which meant murder. There was also the abrupt move to Tucson. Tommy had spent his entire life in Memphis. Yes, he'd toured, he'd traveled to England for a few months hoping to join the music scene in London, but Memphis had been his only true home. There was the connection to this Edward Parker too. The clipping from the newspaper he had sent to Juanita. And lastly, there was the woman both Grace and Bobby had mentioned, a big woman named Liz who drove a white van.

But so much remained hidden. Why was Tommy meeting with Liz? Why was he afraid of her, as Grace said? And what did any of this have to do with Edward Parker? Richard suggested blackmail was involved but it was difficult to imagine a guy like Tommy being part of such a scheme. Tommy was obsessed with Jesus and spirit and mysticism and karma and he wore a yin yang medallion the last years of his life and blackmail would seemingly be against his moral code.

Juanita nodded no. She said they still had so little to go on. Then she said it was important to keep speculation away from fact, and that as much as they speculated, they should also try to remember the firm facts of the situation. They finished their coffee. The lunch crowd had thinned and now the diner was empty except for an elderly couple reading a newspaper by the door. Oscar took the bill, stood slowly from the table. "Guess it's time," he said. Juanita went up with him.

Randy was leaning in the kitchen doorway, laughing and speaking with one of the cooks. When he saw Oscar and Juanita approach he strode up to the counter, taking the ticket. "Ya'll have a good lunch?" he asked as he punched the numbers into the register.

"It was good. Really good." Oscar felt his hands sweating.

He wished he wasn't nervous. He wished he'd not had so much coffee.

"This is out first time here," Juanita said. "We will certainly be back."

"Great to hear," Randy said. He took the twenty Oscar handed him and drew several ones and quarters and nickels from the till.

Oscar glanced at Juanita. Juanita glanced at Oscar. He raised an eyebrow. She raised an eyebrow too. Finally, Juanita said, "I notice your name is Randy. Randy, did you happen to know a gentleman by the name of Tommy Stevens? He used to hang out here, and he mentioned he was friends with a Randy?"

He looked up. "Yes indeed. I know Tommy. How is he doing? I haven't seen him around lately."

Oscar stiffened. This was not what he expected. "He moved to Tucson back in February," he said. "And then he died."

Randy stopped smiling. He glanced behind himself as if to make sure no one stood near him. He lowered his voice. "How did he die?"

Juanita said, "He overdosed on some heroin."

Randy stared at them. His gaze was watchful, neutral. "That's a shame. I realized he had some drug issues but I didn't realize he was doing the hard stuff too."

Oscar said, "But it's more complicated than that. Tommy left us some messages before he died that suggested if he should die it would not be accidental. So we're trying to figure out what all was going on with him these past months, and why he'd suggest such a thing."

Randy handed the change back to Oscar. As he placed it in Oscar's palm he stared into their faces. He did not seem angry or scared. He looked like he was trying to read them, to figure out who they were and how much they knew. He said, "I'm sorry to hear about Tommy. I didn't know him really but the little I did know I liked." He used his chin to gesture toward the front door. "I'm glad you enjoyed your meal. Have a good day."

Juanita said, "Could we talk to you, Randy?"

"I'm working. Don't have time to talk." He banged the register till closed and took a step backwards toward the kitchen door.

"Just some questions," Oscar said. "You don't have to answer a thing you don't want to."

Randy stepped forward, leaning an elbow on the register. "I fully realize I don't have to answer anything I wouldn't want to. I don't know why you'd even bother to say that."

Oscar placed his hands in his back pockets. "I didn't mean it that way. We're trying to figure this thing out. We're not detectives. We're not police. We just want to know the full story."

"Sounds like you know all you need to know. He died from a heroin overdose. If that's what the cops say, go with it."

Oscar glanced at Juanita. Juanita said, "We suspect you know something. We're not trying to get anybody in trouble. We only want to know what happened to our friend."

"Just five minutes of your time," Oscar said.

"I won't be of any help. Like I said, I barely knew him."

"I know," Juanita told him. "We realize that. But if we could talk to you anyway."

Randy sighed and gave them a skeptical but not entirely hostile look and took a brown paper bag from under the counter and scribbled on it and handed it to Juanita. "I'll meet ya'll there, at that time. You two don't show, that's it. No second chances."

Oscar nodded. "We hear you. We'll be there."

Two nights later they drove to the location he'd written on the bag. His instructions said there was a narrow road that linked a shopping center off of Summer Avenue to the drive-in theater further down the street. They were to meet at a spot about halfway down that road where a tree had fallen and now laid on the side of it. They took Oscar's

90

Chevelle. They came up to the side of the tree and waited, the engine idling. Oscar said, "I have a feeling about this."

"A good feeling or a bad one?"

"I can't tell yet."

Further west they could see the big screens standing against the night sky with soundless images flashing across them. One showed a massive space ship hovering over a mountain and another John Travolta in a black T-shirt and greased back hair speaking to a curly hair woman in a fifties car. "You think we're going to be killed out here?" asked Oscar.

"Frank is going to be so mad at you if we are."

"Why would he blame me?"

"Well, he's not going to blame me for doing something so stupid."

"Is this stupid?"

"Yeah, I would say so." She touched the evening purse in her lap. "I brought one of his guns."

"You mean you took it. Borrowing implies you asked him."

"I took it. That's right."

"Have you ever shot a gun in your life?"

"No. And you haven't either. So shut up about it."

Behind them came a rumbling and Oscar looked out the passenger's window and saw a cherry-red Pontiac GTO pull up beside his car. Randy nodded to them. As he pulled up in front and parked on the side of the street Oscar and Juanita got out of the car. Randy walked up carrying a paper bag. "If you two are packing heat, don't worry," he said. "It's just some beers." He dug a hand into the bag, brought out two cans of Miller Lite. He handed one to Juanita and one to Oscar. He dug his hand again into the bag and retrieved one for himself. After he popped open his can and took a sip he looked at the screens in the distance. "Some nights I come out here and get high while watching that shit. Sometimes the stuff on the screen is more interesting when you can't hear what's really going on."

"Thanks for the beer," Juanita said.

"Yeah, thanks."

They both took drinks and walked up to Randy, one on each side of him. He stared at the screen showing a man frantically trying to climb a mountain as helicopters circled around like giant bugs. He took another drink from the can and said, "I met Tommy through this lady named Liz, and I know Liz from New Orleans. That's where I grew up, in New Orleans. My family owns a funeral parlor down there. They've had it for years and years, even back when the city had Storyville going. My grandfather owned a saloon in what they used to call black Storyville. He saw what was coming down the line, he knew the city was getting tired of having all those whorehouses and shit carrying on in the broad light of day, so before the whole thing was shut down he moved what little resources he had and started up a funeral home. It was a black one, of course. Evidently white people don't want black hands on the bodies of their loved ones even in death. God only knows what they think would happen." He laughed, taking another drink.

"Liz was living there?" Oscar asked.

"No, but she did work there. Liz sells drugs. Liz hires herself out as muscle to certain individuals. Liz bugs hotels rooms for wives who want to catch their husbands in certain illicit acts. Liz sells porn for all different appetites. I met her because I was also selling drugs at the time. I used to push weed and pills and crap like that. She would get the merchandise, I would sell it, and then we'd split the profits. Where she was getting the merchandise from I never asked. Now she mainly works in Memphis but back then she was casting a wider net. I think she got tired of being on the road so much."

"You still work with her?" Juanita said.

"I turned my back on it a while ago. I got beat up one night by this other dealer and he robbed all the pills I had on me. Any desire I had to be a pusher man vanished right away that night. But to her credit, Liz stuck up for me. I told her what happened and she didn't ball me out or threaten to do shit to me if I didn't get the pills back. Instead, she asked me what the guy looked like and if I knew where he was from. I knew both and I told her."

Oscar swirled the beer in his can. "What did Liz do?"

"She got it back. The guy was just some loner, didn't have any real connections to anyone or anything bigger. So she didn't have to worry about stepping on toes."

"What'd she do to the guy?"

"What did she not do to him? That would be the question."

Juanita walked around in a semicircle in front of Oscar and Randy. She asked, "What were Liz and Tommy up to together? We've been asking around and it sounds like they might've been in a blackmail scheme. And maybe it involved that city council guy who killed himself around Christmas? Edward Parker?"

Randy stared off at the flickering images on the screens. He gulped down the rest of his beer, crushed the can in his fist. Then he threw the can into the trees and weeds and turned to Juanita. "Here are a few things you should know. The first is, you don't want to miss with Liz. That should be clear. The second is yes, Tommy was involved in a blackmail scheme and that scheme did involve Liz. The third thing is I don't know much outside of that. The fourth goes back to the first, which is you probably don't want to go asking Liz about this shit."

Oscar gazed off at the screens too. "It's hard for me to imagine Tommy blackmailing somebody. The guy I knew was moody and a jerk and depressed as hell most of the time but he also had this sensitive side. I once saw him open a window and try to shoo a fly out of his apartment instead of smacking it with a newspaper as most of us would."

"Drugs and the needs of addiction can do mysterious things to a person," Randy said. He walked behind the fallen tree. Oscar could hear him unzip and piss into the weeds. When he returned, he told them, "I will add this. I lied the other day when I said I didn't know he'd moved out to Arizona. I did know. Liz told me he left Memphis because he thought going out west would help straighten him out. He was going try to stop cold turkey. He had a friend out there, I guess, and he was going to stay with this friend and try to wean himself off the shit. Off the heroin especially. But I was telling the truth when I said I didn't know he'd died. I haven't seen Liz around so I didn't know. But the overdose I think is real. Nobody did him in. And maybe this blackmail shit, maybe it drove him deeper into the drugs. Which would make it a real vicious circle, right? The drugs lead him to do this thing and after he does it he feels so bad he starts taking more drugs. If he was as sensitive to these issues as you say I don't see how he wouldn't start using more."

"Jesus." Oscar rubbed his wrists.

Juanita placed her can on the ground, kicked it with the tip of her shoe into the leaves and darkness.

"I'm sorry." Randy looked at the screens. He looked back at them. "I should get going."

"All right." Oscar took a cigarette from his shirt pocket and lit it. "How come you wanted to meet us out here though?"

"I'm friends with Liz. We've always been on good terms. But I also don't want to advertise the fact we're meeting."

Juanita said, "Can I ask you one last thing about Liz?"

"Sure. I'm not going to give you her address though. And I'm not going to give you her phone number. And I won't for your sake as much as for hers."

"I was wondering why you're still in contact with her even if you don't sell drugs. You two just friends now?"

Randy shook his head, his hands on his hips. "All right, but this is the last question I'm going to answer. I'm getting tired of this." He took a plaid golf cap from his back pocket and put it on his scalp. "I do work with her but in an entirely different capacity. I sell homosexual porn on the side. Porn I get from Liz. It's funny, you can go to Amsterdam Theater up on Summer Avenue and watch a lady like Marilyn Chambers suck cock twenty-four hours a day: but if some guy is sucking off another guy? It has to be circulated in the dark of night. At least it does here in Memphis. I earn most my income doing what you saw me doing the other day. The porn is to have a little extra padding my pockets."

He didn't say goodbye as he walked to his car and closed the door and started the thunderous engine and raced away.

Fourteen

That night, Oscar had plans to meet Brian at Comet Studios on Madison. This would be his first time in the studio since Tommy's death. After he arrived Brian asked how he was doing, and Oscar said he still felt bad for Tommy but the shock was gone. He didn't mention how he'd been going around the city with Juanita, trying to find out more details about the death. Oscar showed Brian the nine by nine print Frank had lent him to use as a possible album cover. Brian said he like how minimalist it was: the red room, the cat tongue-bathing. It visually matched up with the record, which was stark and echoic.

They'd already laid the guitar and drum tracks. Oscar sang the same words into the microphone over and over, trying to get the vocals right. The tile of the song was "Liquid Sky." The lyrics were bits and pieces inspired by rockabilly and blues songs and horror films from the fifties. He threw in some lines about Maria, lines taken from Tommy's journal.

Around one in the morning Oscar looked over at the control room and pointed his thumb down.

Brian pressed a button and leaned forward. He spoke and his voice filled the room. "You want to take a break?"

Oscar raised his thumb up, nodding yes.

They walked out to the back of the studio. It was cool for May. Brain had found a bottle of tequila in the hallway of the studio. He poured some into two Styrofoam cups and handed one cup to Oscar and then slid the bottle into the pocket of his suede jacket. Oscar asked, "You know that boy named Richard that Tommy used to hang out with? The drummer? What do you think of that dude?" He was talking. That was all. He was asking questions because it was cool out and he was tired and starting to get drunk. He felt done with the whole matter: Randy's theory had made sense to both him and Juanita. The drugs leading to debt and the debt leading to a favor and the favor leading to guilt and the guilt leading to more drugs and those drugs leading to Tucson and the desert and death. There was a clear progression now.

Brian shook his head. "Something's off with that guy. Tommy might've been a junkie but he didn't want to be a junkie. Richard, it's not like I know him that well, but when I do, it seems like he enjoys being a junkie. It's his job. It's like a junkie went to his high school on career day and Richard saw him and thought, yeah, that sounds like the life for me."

"Hell of a career. Shit."

"I remember that Sex Pistols show back in January. I remember seeing Richard way up front throwing cups at the band and bouncing up and down and it was like him and Sid Vicious were mirrors. It was eerie how much they looked alike."

"Most people would look pretty much alike if they were gaunt, pale, and had spiky black hair."

"I guess so. I will say this about him, though. He was the only one of us that took the trouble to visit Tommy out there."

"Out in Tucson?" Oscar asked. "He went out there?"

"Yeah. I ran into him at Friday's a few nights after the funeral. He said he'd been out to see Tommy only a few days before he died."

"That's funny. I was talking to him not that long ago. He never brought this up."

"Yeah. He told me he went out there to visit and to take a special package out to him. Then he did that real evil grin like he does. Or at least like he tries to do. He likes to come off as being scary even though he doesn't have much talent

---

97

for it."

Oscar sloshed the tequila around in his mouth. He swallowed. "What was in the package? I imagine he didn't say."

"He didn't. I knew he wanted me to ask so I deliberately didn't ask. Guys like that, it's better to not get wrapped up in their head games."

At two in the morning he drove by Maria's apartment building and saw the lamp near her front windows was still glowing. She had a job waitressing at Luther's Steakhouse on Third Street downtown and often after a shift she was so keyed up she didn't go to bed until sunrise. She was opening the door as Oscar approached. "How did you know I was coming?"

"I have eyes from the back of my head."

"Sometimes I almost believe it."

They took off their clothes beside the low pink sofa. Maria stretched out on the cushions. He knelt down between her legs. After she came he stretched out in the sweaty warm spot where she had been. She knelt down between his legs. After he came, the semen drying on his stomach, he said, "I bet your neighbors are wondering why anybody would be having sex this late on a Thursday night."

"You mean this early on a Friday morning."

She was sitting on the floor with one hand on his leg. He noticed the watch on her wrist, the only item she was wearing. "I don't think I've ever seen you take that watch off."

She looked over at him, smiling. "I know. I never take it off. I'll die with this thing on."

She crawled up on top of him and her body was clammy and cool. "You were at the studio tonight?"

"Yeah. Making more of that music you love to hate."

"If it makes you happy go for it. But don't then turn around and complain when people don't like it."

"You have a point, I guess."

He felt her breathing. A bird was squawking outside and

the thin curtains over the living room windows were lit with the palest of blue lights. Maria told him, "I had a dream last night about Tommy. I was about sixteen years old and he was too and we were both standing by this pond wearing coats. And somehow I knew we both had stones in the pockets of our coats."

Oscar had been stroking her hair but he stopped, resting his hand on her lower back. "You never met Tommy, though."

"That doesn't mean I can't have a dream about him. It also doesn't mean I don't know what he looks like."

"From the album covers."

"Yeah. The album covers."

Oscar swallowed hard, trying to remember the poem fragment about a Maria that Tommy had left in his journal. He said, "Go on."

"This isn't boring you?"

"Not in the least."

"I looked at him and he looked at me, both of us with our hands in our pockets, feeling the rocks we had in them. You know how in a dream it's always hard to tell what time it is? Well, that wasn't the case in this dream. It was early afternoon, just after lunchtime." Her voice was calm and dry, like the voices actors have in films when they're speaking under hypnosis. "Anyway, this boy came out from the woods behind Tommy. Actually, it was this guy, probably in his early twenties. But he looked so thin and small he looked like a boy. He was naked except for this pair of black leather pants. And his hair was black too: real black, like it'd been dyed. And his chest and face were scratched up, like he'd been running through a whole field of thorn bushes. He came out to the edge of the pond and looked at me and then at Tommy and told us it was time. Then we both removed a stone from our pockets. We lifted our arms back like we were going to throw them at one another. But then we threw them at him, this other boy. And they both hit him right in the head, knocking him out cold. And Tommy and I walked up to him and crouched down and we saw this boy wasn't dead or even really hurt, just asleep. And I remember thinking in the dream that'd I'd never seen anyone look so poised and beautiful in their sleep. It was only after I woke up that I realized he looked a lot like you. Except different too. As if running through the woods had done something to your face, made it look just a little different than it is."

Her voice had been growing softer as she spoke and when she stopped speaking after those words he realized she was asleep. He reached up, touching the watch on her wrist. It was icy against his fingertips.

Fifteen

As she worked on the TV in the corner of the room Horace did jumping jacks. Then he did set-ups. He sweated and he grunted. He started jogging in place. He said, "You sure you don't want to join me?" He wore shorts and a long sleeved Kiss T-shirt.

Liz glanced up from behind the TV, a wrench in her hand. "I'm all right. I think exercise is going turn out to be bad for you. Getting your heart going like that, no way is that good."

"Sitting on your ass all day, that's what leads to people getting strokes at twenty."

"How many twenty-year-olds do you know who've had strokes?"

"It makes you ready. That's the main reason I do it."

"Ready for what?"

"Anything that might be out there."

"I'm always ready. I don't need to jog in place to do that." She looked up from behind the TV. "I do lift weights. But I feel like that's part of my work. You need a certain amount of muscle mass in this profession of ours."

"You think that TV is ever going play again?"

"We'll know in a minute."

"How did you get so good at fixing shit?"

"The real question is how come you're so bad at it. I've never known a thirty-year-old man who can fix as little as you."

"I've never been good with my hands, Liz."

"It's your brain that fixes shit, not your hands."

He stopped jogging and paced around the living room, swinging his arms back and forth to cool down. "I'll pay you something even if you don't get it going."

"Don't bother. I'm sure I'll ask for a favor in return someday."

"Just don't expect me to repair something."

"Unless I want something really broke, no, I won't be doing that."

She stood up behind the Sony set. "You want to turn this thing on? Time to see what happens."

Horace walked over to the television and switched it on. A clear picture rolled up showing two wrestlers throwing each other around in the ring. "I'll be damned," Horace said. "You are good. Don't let anybody tell you different."

Later in the afternoon she drove to Methodist Hospital, a bouquet of roses in the seat next to her. It was misting out, the breeze was picking up. By the time she was walking across the parking lot under her umbrella, thunder was rumbling through the sky. This was Richard's third day in the hospital. He'd told her over the phone that he'd blacked out soon after walking into the emergency room and he had not woken up until two hours later. But the main reason the doctors wanted him to stay in the hospital a few days, he'd said, was because of how run-down his body was due to drugs and lack of sleep and piss-poor nutrition. One doctor had told him it was amazing he was walking and talking at all. He'd seen dead people in better condition than him.

Liz handed him the flowers. There was an enormous bandage over his nose. He held the flowers to the nose under those bandages and then placed the roses against his side as if they were a cat or a small dog. "Admit it, Liz. You really came here just to see your handiwork."

He looked small in the bed: small and skeletal. She stroked his foot. "I don't like it when you joke around when I'm trying to be serious."

He laughed. "Guess you really showed me."

"The police visit?"

"I've stuck to the same story since coming here. I tell everyone I threw myself into the wall a few times in fit of rage."

"They know you're lying."

"Of course they do."

She took a plastic cup from the table by the bed and went into the bathroom and poured water into it and returned and took the roses and placed them in the cup and placed the cup back on the table. She brought a chair to his side of the bed. "The doctors and nurses treating you okay?"

"They know I'm a drug addict. I suspect that colors their perceptions. I joke with them but they don't think I'm funny."

"Your sense of humor takes a little getting used to." She patted his wrists and touched his hair. "Bet you haven't been this sober in a long time, have you?"

"They have me on pain meds. That's something at least."

"Good for you. Glad you're getting a little something."

He took her hand from his scalp. He held it. "You know I don't like to ask questions, right? There's a lot about you I don't want to know."

"I think that's smart. More people should be like you."

"But I need to ask you this."

"All right."

He glanced at the door. No one was standing near it. He turned and whispered, "That bag I took with me to Tucson, had it been messed with?"

"Messed with?"

"Was there something in it?"

She leaned back. "Oscar put this idea in your head."

"Yeah. I mean, I know he died a few days after I was there and I know he overdosed and I always suspected, I guess, that he overdosed from the bag we gave him. I mean, that seems likely in terms of the time line."

"It does."

"But what I never thought about was maybe the bag had

been messed with. And if it was, that's not the same as an overdose. It's not even close to the same thing." He really held her hand. He was like a child with a fever wanting reassurance. "You were the one telling me not to touch the shit in that bag. You were the one saying how it was all for Tommy and not to dig into it before giving it to him and how it was extra strong and you didn't think I'd be able to handle it."

"You want the truth? I'll tell you but you have to be sure you want to hear it."

He moved his eyes from her face. Rain pinged loudly against the window. He stared at the pane and the pulses of lightning. Eventually he said, "You know, maybe I should keep to my usual policy about not asking questions. It's worked for me so far."

She pulled her hand from his grip and patted his head. When he started wiping his eyes with his knuckles she took a Kleenex from her pocket and gave it to him.

That night she met Andy at The Shipmate on Forrest Avenue. They split a pitcher on the wooden deck at the back of the building. Black Sabbath played from a jukebox inside, their song "Sweet Leaf." Andy was someone she hired for smaller, less complicated jobs. In his earlier days he'd owned a hardware store on Summer Avenue but he drank too much too keep up with the business. It eventually went bankrupt. Now he did odd jobs for people around town. "It was around four this afternoon when I saw this guy over at Richard's place," Andy was telling her. "I'd been waiting there, watching, for about six hours by then. But you were right. This guy eventually did show up. He banged on the door of Richard's place, looking real pissed. I was watching him with my binoculars and I could see this scowl on his face."

"He was alone? There was no woman with him?"

"Nope. He was alone."

"So you followed him."

"I did. He went to a house only a few blocks from

Richard's apartment. It's right on the corner of North Parkway and South Parkway. It's a fieldstone house tucked away behind shrubs and trees. He picked up this other guy. I reckon he was about my age. And he had on gray slacks and a black turtleneck despite how hot it was today. This older guy put a suitcase in the trunk. I followed them down Airways, toward the airport."

"So Oscar took this guy to the airport?"

"He did. Though there was this weird moment. Their car pulled over in front of this skating rink that was all locked up. It looked like it hadn't been open in years. Anyway, the guy in the turtleneck got out of the car, raised his camera, snapped a picture of the rink, and got back in the car."

Liz stared at him. "Andy, if you could keep with the bigger picture here, that would be great."

"Your buddy Oscar—"

"He's not my buddy. I don't know the guy."

"This fellow Oscar, he drove home after dropping the older guy at the airport. So I have Oscar's address if you want."

"Wonderful. I would every much like that address." She took a small memo book out from the back pocket of her jeans. "Go ahead."

He said the address. He told her, "It's those apartments right across the street from Liberty Land."

"Thank you, Andy. You've come through once again."

In her van she swallowed a Quaalude to soothe her nerves. She placed her head on the back of the seat. The darkness in the van soon began swimming and rippling around her like water and her breath eased and her chest relaxed and the muscles ungripped deep inside her. She saw Oscar on stage in a billowing white shirt and thick beard screaming into a microphone with sweat shinning on his face and Tommy stood behind him clutching his guitar with his shaggy hair over his eyes and his skinny hands flying up and down the strings. There had been a drummer too, though she couldn't remember his name, and she'd heard he moved up to New

York and was playing for different groups up there. She was in the back of the cavernous bar in a black halter-top and bomber jacket, having nailed two men to two planks of wood only the night before.

After taking a brief nap she started the car and made her way east down Poplar Avenue. From Poplar she drove up to Summer Avenue, where there was little traffic, and then on to Baltic. Most of the windows and porches were unlit but there was one house with the porch light on. It was a wooden shack with a porch ceiling that had partially caved in and a BEWARE OF DOG sign tied to a wooden gate leading to the backyard. Liz got out of the van, hefted two large boxes out from the back. As she approached the porch the dog started to bark furiously from behind the gate, the sound so harsh it seemed to rip up the night air around the house. Randy came out to the porch, telling the dog to hush. The animal immediately did, trotting away to someplace further back in the yard. "I could use a hand," Liz said.

Randy walked down the steps and took the top box and they lugged both of them into the house and set them in the center of the living room. The walls were bare and there was no carpet on the floor. The room was silent except for the whirl of the ceiling fan. "It's starting to get hot as a son of a bitch these days," Liz said, wiping her forehead with the bandanna from her back pocket. "Not even the nights are cooling things down much."

"Drink hot tea," Randy told her as he lifted the lids from the boxes. "That helps. At least it does with me."

"I have rotten teeth. Anything hot or cold fucks them up."

Randy crouched down, browsing through the books and film reels in one of the boxes. He took one book out. She saw the cartoon on the cover: a cowboy tied to a tree and a muscled Indian in elaborate headgear fucking him in the ass. The colors in it were rainbow-like and psychedelic. The cowboy had an expression of dumbfounded bliss. "What is it with queers and cowboys?" she asked. "I never understood."

"Shit if I know. Fucking up American's innocent image of

itself? Who knows? I've never been into cowboys."

"What are you into?"

"This will come as a shock to you, but smart, kind, good-looking guys. That's the kind of meat I like in my kitchen." He gestured toward the bottle of Bacardi on the coffee table. "You want a nightcap?"

"No. I took some Quaaludes not long ago. It wouldn't be good to mix." She took a step toward Randy and playfully smacked him on his shoulder and then squeezed his shoulder. "But don't keep me waiting, buddy. Tell me how the meeting went."

"Without a hitch. They bought the I'm-going-to-tell-you-the-real-truth act I gave them. I think you're right. They just want a little information, something to make them feel like they did a favor for Tommy."

"You told them about him and me and the blackmail?"

"Yeah, the stuff the two of us hashed out, the surface shit that doesn't mean much. And I ended with that theory we cooked up about how the blackmail deal led to his final spiral down."

"They seem to buy it?"

"These two don't know shit about police work or detective work. All they know are some movies they might've seen on late night TV."

"Well, I have some bad news, Randy. They didn't buy it. I had a guy watching Richard's place and guess what? Oscar came around there earlier today knocking on the door."

"That so?"

"Yeah, that is so." She took a few steps closer to him, placing her hands on his shoulders and digging in her fingers. They stood with their noses almost touching. "Now why the fuck would he do such a thing if everything went as smoothly as you suggest?"

"I don't know. I really don't."

"Look at me. Look me right in the eyes."

"I am looking at your fucking eyes. What the fuck else am I supposed to look at?"

They stared hard into one another. "Did you fuck up?"

"No."

"Did you?"

"I really thought they'd let it drop. I really did."

She stepped away from him. She rested her elbow on the doorjamb and scratched the back of her head. "Okay. All right."

"What the hell would you think I would tell them? Jesus Christ. You need to calm down."

"You're in this too. You should be more nervous."

Randy picked the bottle of Bacardi up from the table and drank from the bottle and wiped his mouth with the back of his free hand and looked at Liz. She said, "Don't give me that fucking look. I'm still not entirely convinced you didn't let something out by accident."

"I am nothing if not discreet."

"You better be." As Liz walked over toward the door, she said, "You hear from Diana?"

"I did, about a week ago. She wrote me a letter. It wasn't long. She's in New York still but she wants to move to Berlin."

"What's in Berlin?"

"Her dude. Or one of them. This army guy she met up there."

"It's funny how all this shit revolves around her and she's not even here. Those letters she writes, are they discreet as you are?"

"Of course, Liz. Why do you go around assuming everyone is stupid?" He took another drink from the Bacardi, closing the door as she left.

Sixteen

Oscar was sitting in a recliner in his underwear with his headphones on listening to the first record by Cosmic Dust, an album called Up High that for its cover showed Tommy standing barefoot on the hood of a rusted beat-up truck with a bat behind his neck and his two arms hanging from both sides of that bat and the sun setting into the row of shaggy mimosas behind him. He remembered the day of the picture and how Frank had driven him and Tommy and Stewart the drummer out to Frank's family's plot of land outside Clarksdale and how Tommy talked the entire drive down about how the songs should be sequenced on the record and Frank smoked and barely said a word and he himself was hung over from a party the night before, big sunglasses covering his eyes. He was sitting in the recliner with the fan spinning in the corner, blowing cool air on his feet and up his legs, and he was now listening to "Ballad of the Gunslinger" with Tommy doing the backup vocals and Oscar using one of his thicker, denser singing voices, the lyrics describing a gunslinger riding through dusty roads flanked by tropical foliage until he reaches a cemetery where wild cats are frolicking, and he stops his horse to watch the cats, and only as the ash begins to drift from the sky and settle along his coat and sombrero does he realize he is dead, a corpse laid out on a bar in Oklahoma City with candles at his feet and head. It was a song they had written together, him and Tommy. It was the spring of seventy-one and they were in Tommy's place which was a room above the garage behind Tommy's aunt's house on Peabody Avenue. There was honeysuckle growing on a fence near the garage, he could smell it as they worked at the kitchen table on the song, and he could smell it now, here, as he sat in this recliner. Tommy paced around in his T-shirt and flared jeans talking about how he liked the image of ash falling from the sky, he occasionally even saw it in dreams, and he liked the idea of the gunslinger being lost in this rain of ash, his realization that he'll never stride among the living again. And one year later Tommy came up with a kind of sequel for the "Ballad of the Gunslinger." It came to him on the tour bus as they drove through Ohio at four in the morning. When Oscar woke up Tommy was there in the seat next to him, humming a few bars, telling him how in this new song the main guy would be a delinquent greaser who'd been on the run for years and who tries to return to his home town but can't, the maps are never quite right, the directions he gets from people at gas stations lead him only to cornfields and Baptist churches, but finally he sees the cemetery he remembers from the town, and he speeds towards it, he's finally almost home, but nothing is there past the cemetery, there are only more fields behind the cemetery, and he stops the car and gets out and takes off his shoes and walks through the soggy grounds of the cemetery trying to read the weather-worn names and hoping to find some that are familiar. And Cosmic Dust did wind up recording this sequel, the song would be the seventh one on their second album Low. But by then Tommy kept threatening to quit the band. Cosmic Dust had been Tommy's idea and Tommy had been the one to approach him in the months after Toy Soldiers had blown apart when Oscar started taking a few classes at Memphis State and Tommy sat at his table in the dinning hall and asked aren't you the singer from Toy Soldiers? And after Oscar explained how the band had fallen apart Tommy had said he was trying to start a band of his own, a group inspired by the Beatles and a whole bunch of

British shit but also by soul music and the stuff coming out from Stax Records. Then Oscar said for Tommy to give him his number and yeah, he might be interested, because he really loved British shit and Stax too. The first months the band consisted of the two of them. At Tommy's place they would strum guitars and sit on pillows smoking dope and listening to Abbey Road and Otis Redding singles, analyzing the vocal inflections and the note changes and why some worked and why some just blew your fucking head off. And it was so different from Toy Soldiers because back then Oscar and the other members were sixteen and seventeen and they were horny and they wanted to get famous and they discussed music in terms of how to get girls and get attention. What was doing well on the charts? Let's sound like those motherfuckers! That had been the attitude, and he'd been a big part of that attitude. But with Tommy the music wasn't about getting the masses to adore you, wasn't about trying to get a blonde seventeen-year-old to spread her legs for you. It was about trying to reach someone specific, a long hair girl looking out her window on a stormy day, a heavyset boy wearing all black and reading Rimbaud by flashlight in his backyard at night. And yet, that hadn't been all of it, at least not for Tommy. With Toy Soldiers Oscar knew fame and he'd faced a crowd of thousands screaming the titles of his songs. Tommy claimed he didn't want that shit but he did, on some level he did, and when their first album Up High came out in stores Oscar could see how Tommy thought he was about to be catapulted to new exciting territories and give shows to huge crowds and maybe meet his idols like Brian Wilson and Paul McCartney along the way. Tommy would say in those weeks before the record's release we're going to be big whether we like it or not. And he had a glint in his eyes Oscar had never noticed before, a light of feverish expectation. But the record didn't make them the new Beatles. It didn't even make them the new Toy Soldiers. Their tour consisted mostly of bars in the South and Midwest where a few dozen fans would show up among the tables. That was when Tommy started snorting coke and dropping acid and talking about God and angels and mystics and how very few people realized the truth about this world but he was determined to be in their number. After the tour, and when they were back in Memphis, Oscar would call Tommy but his phone would be off the hook, and he'd drive out to the garage over which Tommy lived and throw stones at the window and Tommy would finally appear at the glass and raise the window and say he had a cold or a headache and didn't feel like hanging out that day. When two or three months passed, though, Tommy began venturing out again. It was fall of seventy-two. He said I'm going to break their hearts this time. I want us to do some songs that'll make every one of those fuckers cry. I want them to drown in their fucking tears. So they started sitting around in Tommy's room again smoking weed, jotting down lyrics. It was Tommy's idea to call the album Low. He said he maybe the title Up High had been a kind of curse, pride goeth before the fall and all that shit. But during the sessions at Ardent Recording Studio in the first weeks of seventy-three, Oscar felt himself and Stewart drifting away from the sonic landscape Tommy was trying to create. Tommy wanted to make Up High again, with its harmonies and crystal clear guitar work, but Oscar and Stewart wanted to bring in a harsher, more atonal element, the two of them were listening to a lot of Velvet Underground and Iggy Pop and Sly and the Family Stone's There's a Riot Goin' On and that type of frenzied, muddied lurching felt right to them, felt like the next step they wanted Cosmic Dust to take. They started to argue about it with Tommy, real nasty fights. One night after a recording session, while the three of them were drinking at the Friday's in Overton Square, Tommy said he thought the record was starting to sound like crap, you couldn't hear the drums from the guitar from the vocals, it was all one big sloughing sonic sludge, and Oscar said better that than trying to sound all pretty like a group from the mid-Sixties, and Tommy had said fuck you and Oscar said fuck you, and the tables around them grew quiet, and Stewart laughed and said you two boys calm down now, the studio session is over, remember? Then Tommy picked up his glass of beer and drank the whole thing in a few gulps and left. In the next few weeks Tommy showed up to the studio less and less. When he was there he barely talked. When he did talk it was usually a simple yes or no. Then there was a stretch of days when he didn't show at all. Three days, and four, and five, and then a week. Oscar drove over to his place, threw pebbles at the window until Tommy raised the glass up. He asked if Tommy was done. Tommy said yeah, count him out of Cosmic Dust, it just wasn't his band anymore. And Oscar said all right, but it would be final, he couldn't show up in the studio one night if he changed his mind, and Tommy said not to worry, he wouldn't be changing his mind. That very day, Oscar told the guitarist who'd been filling in for Tommy that he could be the new member of Cosmic Dust if he wanted to be, and he did.

Oscar got out of the recliner, turned the music off. He looked out the window at the parking lot to the side of his apartment building. The red Ford truck he'd seen earlier that night remained there at the far side of the lot. The red bud of a lit cigarette glowed whenever the figure inside the truck inhaled from it. But the truck was too distant for him to be able to tell who the figure was and what the figure might be looking at. Oscar took a T-shirt and jeans from the floor of his bedroom and tugged them on and placed his keys in his jeans and lifted the front window that faced the street and not the parking lot and crawled out. He went down to the sidewalk, skirting the apartment building and making a long C up into the driveway of the parking lot. He hid behind a dumpster and peered out from the corner. A balding man with a thick goatee sat smoking in the truck. He was looking to his left, at Oscar's apartment door. His radio played "If I Didn't Care" by the Ink Spots.

Oscar moved back behind the dumpster, sitting with his

back against it. He rubbed his eyes and the back of his head and sighed. "I can't believe this shit," he muttered. He touched his lip and his eyebrow. They were still tender from the fight with Richard. There were a row of houses across from the parking lot but they none of them had lights on. It was almost one in the morning. They were probably in bed. But if the confrontation became bad enough, Oscar figured, he could scream loud enough to wake some of the inhabitants of those houses.

As he stood he kept in a crouched position. He darted to the bed of the truck and crept around the side to the cab and grabbed the handle and pulled the door open and took the shirt front of the man sitting there who dropped his cigarette in surprise. Oscar yanked at the shirt collar with both hands. But instead of pulling the man out of the car he simply tore the buttons out of his shirt off. The man sent his arms flying forward, his hands grasping for Oscar's neck, but Oscar took him by the wrist and pulled him out and the man landed hard on his knees and before he could even turn his head up to look at him Oscar kicked him in his side with his pointy-toed cowboy boot. The man curled into himself. "All right, I give. I give, man."

Oscar said, "Why the hell are you watching my door?"

"I'm getting paid to do it, what do you think? I'm not sitting out here jacking off or some shit like that."

"And who's paying you?"

"Usually the way these things work, you're not supposed to tell. It's implied in the agreement."

"You want me to kick the shit out of you again?"

"I'd rather have to deal with you than her."

"Liz?"

The man chuckled. "Shit, so you already know her."

"I don't know her at all. But I've heard a lot about her these past few days." He reached his hand out and the man looked at it suspiciously and Oscar waited and the man took it and Oscar helped him up. "Back in the day," the man said, "I would've had your ass on the ground and your hands and feet all hog-tied."

"Glad we're not back in those days then." He picked up the three white buttons he saw on the black asphalt and handed them to the man. The man took them, thanked him. Oscar said, "You tell Liz I don't like being followed and I don't like being watched. Tell her also that I'd like to set up a time to meet with her. Tell her I'm not trying to stir shit up, I just want to talk."

"Will do. You mind if I tell her I kicked your ass, though? That you came up to me and I beat the living daylights out of you and only as I was leaving you said you wanted to talk to her?"

"Whatever floats your boat, man."

The door of the truck was still open and the man pulled himself up into the driver's seat. "You know, Liz must like you for some reason."

"Why would you say that?"

"This is between the two of us, but she has partners who, if they knew what you were doing, would grind you down to dust in a heartbeat. The fact you're alive at all tells me she must be watching out for you. Liz thinks I'm too dumb to notice such things. But she's wrong. I only look dumb."

Oscar waved to the man as he drove off. He walked up to the dumpster and watched until the tail lights of the truck had vanished down the road and then he bent over and got sick.

In his apartment he turned out the lights and took a sleeping pill and went to bed with his boots and clothes on. In the morning he drove west down Union Avenue, over to Juanita's apartment building. The vestibule with its cracked yellow tiles smelled like cooking cabbage. He walked up the creaky stairs with its dingy red carpet and chipped banister and knocked on the first door of the landing. Juanita opened the door and looked at his face. She didn't say anything. Then she said, "What's wrong, Oscar?"

They spoke on the balcony. A white hair woman in a peasant blouse was pulling weeds in the courtyard below.

Oscar described the night before. He said, "You should go up to New York and visit your dad."

"I'm not the one being followed."

"You don't know that."

"I'm pretty sure I do. You don't have any more experience with being followed than I do. And if someone as lacking in the awareness of his surroundings as you could figure it out, I'm sure I could too."

"Just go to New York until I talk to Liz."

"I want to talk to her too."

"Frank would fucking kill me."

"You're scared of Frank?"

"Not in the least. But I like him, and I don't want to go behind his back with this stuff."

"What are you talking about, Oscar? We've been going behind his back with this stuff since the night of Tommy's funeral."

Oscar lit a cigarette, placed one hand on the iron railing of the balcony. The woman in the courtyard stood by the birdbath, filling it with clean water from her watering can. "I'm not going anywhere," Juanita said, and she went back inside.

Seventeen

The phone rang a few minutes after seven in the morning. An unfamiliar male voice said she should meet Vince in the back of St. Anthony's Church at precisely four in the afternoon and hung up. After the call she took out the phone book to write down the address of the church. It was at Adams Avenue and Third Street, near the river and in a neighborhood where some of the city's oldest houses stood.

She walked in at four exactly and saw an elaborate altar of huge-winged angles and flowing robes and a gaunt, long-armed and crucified Jesus all entirely in white as pristine as spun sugar. The glossy wooden pews were empty, and there was no one around the altar either, though several lit votive candles affixed to the different corners of the church gave off a warm glow in the blue air of that space. The door opened behind her. Vince walked in, alone. He held his fedora in his left hand and with his right he dipped his fingers in the holy water at the entrance and made the sign of the cross. As he walked down the aisle he nodded to Liz. He took a seat in one of the back pews, under a stain glass window that threw patches of gold and blue on them and the pew. She sat next to him. Vince whispered, "It's always quiet here."

"It is that."

"Churches are the last real place for privacy. But I don't think it'll last long. In New Orleans, assholes keep breaking in and stealing chalices or even the bottles of wine from the sacristy. Say what you will about my tribe, at least we have a sense of respect." He crossed his legs, looked over at her. "Don't be nervous."

She grinned. "Isn't that what they say in the movies when some real bad shit starts to go down?"

Vince laughed. "I guess they do. Though I've never been much of a film buff. Music is more my thing, Glenn Miller and those guys." The doors of the church opened and a young woman of about thirty entered, carrying a vase of tulips. She wore a silver cross and looked like she might be a nun. Vince sat up. "Miss, my friend and I here are having an important and private discussion. Would you mind returning in ten minutes?"

The woman stared, clearly surprised by the request.

Vince stood. "Ten minutes, all right? I don't think that is too much to ask." He stood and gestured to the door.

She left, her shoes clicking against the floor.

As Vince sat down, he said, "I imagine I should make this quick. There might be others coming in soon, you never know. Here's the situation. It has come to my attention that some of the pictures we took of Edward Parker have seen the light of day. An associate of mine in New York says some of the pictures got printed up in a book that's been circulating. You know anything about this, Liz?"

"I don't." And she didn't. She'd had a manila envelope with one print of the photographs but she burned them in one of the freestanding grills on the eastern side of Overton Park. She'd filled it with charcoal, lit up a huge fire. Then she'd placed the envelope on the flames and watched as they curled and blackened and whitened and turned ash. She gazed into Vince's face. "I really honestly don't know how that could happen. I destroyed the pictures I had just like we were supposed to after he died."

"And who else had copies?"

"One of the guys who works for me, Randy Collins, he knew a guy with a photo lab. We paid him to print the pictures. We told him to only make three sets. One for me, and one for Horace, and one to give to Edward Parker himself."

"Do you know for certain Horace burnt his set?"

"I can't imagine he wouldn't."

"There are reasons why this bothers me. Edward Parker had a big name locally and if the right people got hold of one of these books with the compromising pictures of him, we could have a real headache on our hands. All we need is for some journalist trying to make a name for himself to start investigating the story behind those pictures. That would not be fun."

"It certainly would not."

"And journalists, it's dangerous to get rid of them. They're like mosquitoes. You slap one and there are ten more ready to take its place. Also, there's a certain amount of sloppiness about this. Mr. Parker paid what we asked of him. Why he killed himself is between him and his God but he settled things with us. Because of this we should do right by him. I know that sounds hypocritical considering what we did to the poor son of a bitch but it's true. We are a business and a business honors its promises. If it doesn't, all you have is chaos and a bunch of barbarians at your door."

The young woman came in again, her shoes tapping against the floor, echoing up in the high ceiling. She still held the vase. She said to Vince, "I need to put these on the altar. I have to get to work."

Vince said, "Get out. Give us one more minute."

"No," she said. She looked about to cry.

Vince sighed, shrugged. "All right then. Do whatever the fuck you have to do. But don't listen to us."

She walked quickly up to the altar, placing the tulips under the statue of Mary holding a fat baby Jesus. Vince continued. "You're wondering why I'm talking to you and not Horace. I know you're wondering even if you don't want to ask me outright. It's because I consider you a serious person. Horace always strikes me as a guy who wants everyone to think he's cooler than he is. He tries too hard, like when he wears sunglasses inside, or the way he smirks when you talk to him. You have all that black leather shit but it's different. You're a woman and I know you have to present a certain demeanor. But beneath it I sense you're serious. You want more in this life than simply trying to be the hippest asshole in the room."

As Vince talked Liz watched the woman at the front of the church kneel and pray in front of Mary. "I'll ask around," she said. "I'll find out what happened."

"I knew I could trust you."

On the way home she picked up a box of fried chicken and coleslaw at the Popeye's next to the Amsterdam Theater and ate one of the chicken legs on the ride back to the green-shingled bungalow she rented on Young Avenue. As she drove up she saw Andy's truck out front. She parked and wiped her fingers clean with a napkin and walked up to Andy who was walking toward her. "He found out I was watching him and tried to rough me up but I beat the hell out of him."

"I'm sure you did, Andy. So he found out?"

"He found out. He wants to talk to you."

"That's nice. I guess I want to talk to him." She wiped her lips with the napkin. "This Edward Parker shit just keeps rolling and rolling. When the guy killed himself, I thought all right, that's over with. I was so very wrong about that."

"He was an important guy. It was a risk, what you all were doing."

"I never even wanted to. It was Horace and Randy. They had the idea and Horace was the one to discuss it over with Vince's people." She placed her arm around Andy's shoulder, gave him a tight squeeze. "I know you don't like dirty work but you're going have to help me out tonight. I need to take care of something. You're okay with that, right?"

"Well, Barbra said…"

"You can call Barbra from inside the house here. You tell her you're going to be a little busy."

Eighteen

He went up to Maria's door and again she opened it right as his hand was about to knock. "I swear, you're a magician," he said.

"You're a loud walker. I hear you on the landing."

He walked in and saw a mirror with two lines of coke on it and a bottle of wine next to the mirror with two mugs beside it. "It would make a beautiful still life, don't you think?" Maria said.

They snorted the coke, they drank some of the wine, they made out on the pink sofa. The apartment felt even cooler than usual. As Oscar took off the T-shirt, he asked, "How do you keep it so cool in here this time of year? It's like you're living in a different season from the rest of us."

"Maybe I am."

They made out for several more minutes. Then she abruptly moved away from him. "I'm thirsty," she said quietly. She took a drink of the wine and placed the mug back on the coffee table. She then sat back into the cushions of the sofa, staring at the wall in front of her. Oscar looked over at her. "You got something on your mind?"

She nodded, standing and walking a little away from him and picking up her mug and drinking. "I need to be honest with you. I knew Tommy growing up."

"What? What are you talking about?"

"I knew him. I've been pretending I haven't."

"How did you know him?"

She took another drink. The room felt cooler now than when he first came in. She said, "I didn't know him that well but I did know him. I lived with my mom in Como for two years. This was before we moved back here. She wanted to get away from the city and all the crime so she moved us down to Como where I had an aunt."

"Tommy would spend some of his summers there at his grandparents' place when he was growing up."

"That's right. That's how I met him."

Oscar smiled. "I knew something was going on. A few days ago his dad gave me some of his notebooks to look at and one of them had this poem about a girl named Maria. I read it and thought about you. Not just because of the name though, and the fact she had dark hair in the poem. Something else. Just this sense, this vibration."

Oscar started to shiver. He put his shirt back on. "You have something else you want to tell me," he said. "I can feel it."

"There is." She placed her mug on the table, next to the mirror. "Does it seem like you're dreaming?"

"No."

"Does it seem like you're awake?"

"No. Not that either." He laughed. "Was there something extra special in that coke?"

"No. It was the same it's always been." She started walking in circles in the middle of the dining room. He listened but he didn't hear her feet against the floorboards: no creaking, no padding of her soles against the bare wood. She said, "I know you've noticed my watch before. Have you ever looked at it closely?"

He shook his head. He edged forward on the sofa, placing his elbows on his knees. She held the arm with the watch up and with her free hand removed her it, putting it carefully on the table. It had no numbers or hands: there was a blank white oval behind the glass. "It would be extra hard to tell time with a watch like that, wouldn't it?" she asked.

"Yes it would be. I hope you didn't pay too much for it."

She stroked his hair. "I paid a lot for it. I paid so much. Can you believe that? I paid a lot for a watch that doesn't even tell you the time. At least a broken watch is right twice a day." She stopped stroking his head and walked over to the bedroom door and opened it. A gust of cool air drifted out and washed over him. She asked, "Are you ready?"

"Not even a little." He took another large gulp from his mug, stood, and joined her at the door.

She led him through her bedroom, where the lamps were off and the bed was made and where a moth fluttered by a window lit from a streetlamp outside. There was a door at the far end of the room. He had never seen this door in the bedroom before but it was possible he simply never noticed it: they always made love and slept on the sofa, not the bed. Red light shined along the sides of the door. She touched the doorknob and turned to him. "We can't stay here long."

"I'm fine with that," he told her.

Inside an amber light shined and wires hung along the walls and pictures hung on pegs from the wires. Yet this was very different from Frank's darkroom. Unlike Frank's, there were no dirty coffee cups setting on counters, no dog-eared paperbacks scattered on tables, no half-eaten sandwiches rotting in the trashcan. This place was pristine, spotless. Oscar looked at the pictures and realized they were all of Maria and Tommy standing by a pond. In every one they had mud on their cheeks and foreheads. They looked sixteen, seventeen. At the very back of the room hung a crimson velvet curtain. Maria led him by the wrist to it and pulled the cloth back. Behind was the space of a walk-in closet. A naked amber light bulb hung from the ceiling. Tommy was perched on a stool under the bulb with his shoulders hunched and his eyes on the ground. He looked up and said, "Hey, Oscar. You come here to take a picture of me?"

Oscar felt too numb to say anything. He took a deep breath and answered, "I didn't know you were back here to take a picture of."

Tommy rubbed his shins vigorously with his hands. "It's all right, man. I'm tired of the pictures anyway. Every time I start to relax they tell me it's time to go out and have a few more pictures taken."

"Who is 'they'?"

"The ones always taking us out to the pond. You'll meet them at some point, I guess. They don't say a lot."

Oscar stared at Tommy. Tommy stared back. Oscar said, "You're dead, Tommy. You know that, right?"

"I guess I do. I remember being in Arizona. I remember I used to take walks in the desert right at sunset. I knew I didn't have long."

"How did you know?"

"I never should've taken that photography class at Memphis State. If I could go back that'd be the one thing I'd change. That, and having Frank help me with my photography chops the few times we hung out."

"I didn't know you two ever hung out. And I didn't know you even had a camera." He looked behind his back and saw Maria roaming around the darkroom, glancing at the photographs on the pegs.

"You don't remember me taking pictures from the bus when we were on tour?"

"A little, I guess. I was doing the same thing with my Polaroid."

Tommy stood from the stool. He was taller than he had been in life. He looked about eight feet and his head touched the ceiling. "They would've had me do it anyway, of course. Hiding in the closet. Then springing out. Taking those pictures. I knew he didn't treat her right and I figured it was okay because of that. What I was doing was bad but it wasn't like this guy was some saint. Anyway, that was the story I told myself beforehand. But it was different, afterwards. Even though I think it was her idea, I still felt like shit afterwards. And I don't think she liked it either. I don't think she knew what it'd be like, having her picture taken that way. That very night, you could see it. At least I felt like I could. A sort of sadness and regret."

"Who's 'she'?"

"Diana."

"Do I know her?"

"She moves around a lot. Everybody meets her eventually." He rubbed is midriff with his hand. "Oscar, could you do me a huge favor? If you run into her, tell her I'm sorry."

"Where is she?"

"I don't know. All I can say is, sometimes when you turn around, she's right there, as if she somehow knew you were looking for her. Tell her I'm sorry. You don't have to go into detail. Just that I'm sorry."

Oscar was about to ask another question about her. But Maria was leading him away by the wrist. The velvet fell back across the doorway and the door to the darkroom itself closed as soon as they stepped from it. The next morning Oscar opened his eyes and rose up from the sofa. Tucked into the corner of the mirror on the table was a note that read I HAD TO GO TO CLASS. YOU WERE SLEEPING SO SOUNDLY I DID NOT WANT TO WAKE YOU. LOCK THE DOOR WHEN YOU LEAVE. LOVE, MARIA. Across the mirror was her watch. He picked it up and glanced at the Roman Numerals and moving second hand. After he placed it back over the mirror he quickly dressed. He thought about going into the bedroom to see if there really was another door in there. But he didn't, grabbing his keys and leaving instead.

When he arrived at his apartment he showered and shaved and took a Quaalude and gulped down a glass of seltzer water. He called Juanita. He told her, "If something should happen to me, remember this name: Diana."

"What's this about?"

"Just keep it in mind."

When he hung up he realized he was not along in the kitchen. A woman of about three hundred pounds stood in the arched doorway. She had short blond hair and white driving gloves. "Liz," he said.

"Your truly."

"Can we talk?"

"We sure can. But not here."

"Where then?"

That was when the hood came down over his head and he smelled a sweet but faintly chemical scent and then nothing.

When he came back to himself he realized he was in a van. The hood had been removed from his head. His hands and feet were braceleted by handcuffs and his waist was tied to the car seat with a chain. He couldn't move his lips. He raised his hand and felt masking tape. In front of him in the driver's seat sat Liz. Next to her in the passenger's seat was the man he'd encountered at his apartment the night before last. Liz glanced up in the driver's mirror and their eyes met. "Look who's coming back to life, Andy," she said.

Andy turned, waved at him.

Oscar groaned. Under the tape he was telling them to go fuck themselves. But what he said came out only as groans and mumbles.

"Andy said he roughed you up real good," Liz told him. "But you don't look that roughed up to me. Could it be Andy here was maybe exaggerating just a tad?"

Oscar glared at them.

Liz looked in the mirror, their eyes meeting again. "Doesn't matter, in the long run. I'm glad we're finally going to have an opportunity to talk. I've been thinking a lot about you the past few days."

Oscar glared at them.

"Honey, we'll fix that soon as we get to where we're going. You sit back and enjoy the ride until then. You should at least be happy we don't have a bag over your head to keep you from seeing where we're going. When we have guests, that's usually what we do. But you strike me as a good, decent, reasonable person. So we'll forgo the hood, all right?"

Oscar turned his head. Out the side window he saw trees

flash by and a few cows on the hill far from the road.

After an hour of driving they reached a sign that welcomed them to Choctaw County, and soon they reached the border of Johnson. They drove past the grocery store and Laundromat and post office and were soon passing branches and fields again. Then they took a left, going east along a gravel road. Trees and shrubs closed in around the van forming a greenleafed tunnel that would occasionally give way to brief views of a valley with a few standing puddles of water. The van came up toward a gate. Andy climbed out of the van, unlocked the padlock, swung the gate open, and climbed back into the van. As soon as they were past the gate Oscar glimpsed the house. It was red-bricked and two-storied and from one side of the porch hung an American flag and from the other hung a Confederate. Closed white curtains covered most of the windows. Liz glanced at him again in the mirror. "We're here, Oscar. Aren't you excited?"

This time he didn't groan. He just stared at her.

Chapter Nineteen

Liz unshackled Oscar and had him go in front of her into the kitchen. Walking behind him, she was struck by how much he looked like Tommy from behind. The hair was completely different. Tommy had black hair and Oscar was dirty blonde. But they both had thin backs and long legs and both walked with a poised deliberation that maybe came from spending time on stage, in the eyes of others. Andy was already in the kitchen as they came in. He was getting the pork chops out of the refrigerator, the skillet from the pantry. He'd become friends with Jimmy over the years and he knew where things were in the house. Liz said, "Andy's going to fix us something to eat. Let's sit in the living room and talk a bit until then."

Oscar pointed to the tape over his mouth.

Liz said, "I almost forgot." She grabbed a washcloth from the bathroom off from the kitchen and told him to wetten the tape with it and then start pulling. As he did so they went into the living room, which always smelled of mold, and sat in two wooden chairs arranged by the windows looking into the backyard. In that yard Jimmy was cutting back some shrubs with a pair of garden sheers. He was shirtless and his shoulders were blotchy red. Oscar finished working the tape off his face. He flung it on the floor and gave her a Fuck You look. "You know, being kidnapped isn't a great way to start off a conversation," he said. "Just to let you know."

"It's not kidnapping. You're going to get back to your

apartment after this. We're just borrowing you. Think of it that way."

"So I'm free to go if you want?"

"No, Oscar. Because we aren't done borrowing you." Liz sat back, crossing her legs with her ankle on her knee. "You want a cigarette?"

"I would love one."

"Andy!" she called into the kitchen. "Andy, could you bring our friend here a cigarette? It's a long ride from Memphis to Choctaw County."

Andy entered the room holding out a pack. He threw it at Oscar and Oscar caught it, slid one out from the packet. His hands were shaking. He took a lighter from the pocket of his jeans and Andy returned to the kitchen. Liz said, "I saw you perform once. You and Tommy both."

"Really? That's great."

"It's going to be hard to talk to you if you're so fucking snide."

Oscar looked up at her, bringing his shaky hand with the cigarette in it up to his mouth and inhaling. Part of her wanted to reach out and rub his back and tell him it would be okay. But of course she didn't.

She told him, "I saw Cosmic Dust play in that same place where the Sex Pistols played back in January. What's it called?"

"The Taliesyn Ballroom. How were we?"

"You were great. You weren't no Rolling Stones or anything but you were good."

"You've heard the Rolling Stones live?"

"In Chicago once back about seven or eight years ago. You?"

"I have. And I met Keith Richards. We hung out one night in New York back when I was with the Toy Soldiers."

"Lucky you."

Oscar blew smoke from his mouth at her with another Screw You expression and shrugged and tapped ash out through the open window. Liz stood and took a step toward him. She slapped him across the face. She was careful to hold back, not use her full strength. Oscar fell from the chair with cigarette ash drifting in the air around him as it tumbled to the floor too. As he leaned forward and coughed she reached down and picked the cigarette up from the carpet and waited for him to get back in the chair. Oscar held the side of his face, gave her another Fuck You glance. But this time there was more hurt and fear in it. He carefully stood and tugged his shirt back down, staring at her face the entire time. Only then did he reach out and take the cigarette. "You could beat the shit out of me in a second," he said, sitting back down. "But if you think that's going to make me somehow respect you then you really are mistaken."

"Just stop with the goddamn attitude, all right?"

She sat back down, crossing her legs again. "You know what my favorite record was? The best thing I think you ever did? I'm talking about Cosmic Dust here, not the Toy Soldiers. I always thought the shit you did with that group was pretty dumb. But Cosmic Dust, the best thing you guys ever did was Big Black Chevelle. That last record. Now that was a really good record. I used to play it over and over. Nobody liked it, I guess, but I liked it."

"Some critics liked it, just not our fans. The few dozen fans we had out there, at least." He inhaled from his cigarette. "It was my favorite too. You're right. It's the best thing I ever did."

Andy came in from the kitchen, said the food was ready.

The three of them took seats at the small round kitchen table. There was a pot of coffee in the middle of the table and a jar of applesauce and a tub of coleslaw and a platter of pork chops. Oscar stared at the food. He kept his hands on the sides of his plate. He told them, "I'm not really all that hungry, to tell you the truth."

Liz assured him, "Why would we give you food if we were going to turn around and kill you?" She looked at Andy and they both laughed. "Shit, that wouldn't make much sense. If we were going to kill you you'd be dead already, not sitting here with us like this."

Andy leaned forward, grinning. "Yeah, and there'd be one more pork chop for me."

They laughed again.

She watched closely as Oscar slowly forked a pork chop from the platter over to his plate. She said, "Go ahead and ask whatever you want to ask. I'll answer what I can."

Oscar was dabbing applesauce on top of his pork chop. "Did you or somebody you know kill Tommy?"

"Wow. You really go straight to the point."

He took a sip of coffee, looking up at her.

She raised her hands, palms facing Oscar. "These hands did not kill Tommy, I absolutely promise you that."

"Was he killed by someone else?"

Liz remembered her last telephone conversation with Tommy. She was in her living room and Tommy in his Tucson apartment and she could hear Richard in the background, humming the way he did when he was high off speed. She asked Tommy if Richard had given him the special package and he said Richard had and she said you should only try it if you think you can handle it and Tommy said he understood and would think about it. She'd added that the package was a gift and he should only use it if he promised he was done with his threats. And Tommy said yeah, yeah, Richard had explained everything. She chewed and swallowed and told Oscar, "He put that needle into his own arm. Nobody did it for him and nobody was holding a gun to his head to make him do it. This I promise."

"How were you and Tommy mixed up with Edward Parker?"

"Did Richard tell you this?"

"Tommy did, in his cryptic way."

"Edward Parker was that type of southern gentleman obsessed by black pussy. He felt black pussy was his right and his heritage. Tommy and myself and others I won't name blackmailed him about it. I won't go into any further details."

131

"That's why he ended up killing himself? Because of the blackmail?"

"He paid us what we wanted him to pay us. So I'm not sure why he killed himself."

"Maybe he thought you might return, blackmail him some more."

"Maybe. I don't know what was running through his mind."

"But it does seem pretty far out there, don't you think? Killing himself over it? I mean, he wouldn't be the first politician around here in a sex scandal. Down in New Orleans they seem to even take pride in them."

Liz cut into her pork chop. "I can't go into any more details."

Oscar started to pour another cup of coffee Liz noticed his hands were not trembling quite as much. Andy continued to eat wordlessly. Liz said, "Why do you care so much?"

"If you had a friend who you think might've killed, wouldn't you care? Wouldn't you try to figure out what happened?"

"But the rumor was you and Tommy weren't even that close. And that when he left Cosmic Dust there was some real bad blood between you."

"That's true. But for a few months, we were close. When we did that first album and went on that tour, we were almost like brothers."

"That was years ago."

"Doesn't mean it didn't happen."

"Fair enough, I reckon."

As she took a sip from her coffee she heard steps outside the house. She glanced over at the window behind Tommy's shoulder and saw Walter standing there, aiming his rifle at her. "Get down!" she yelled, moving below the table and reaching for the gun at the back of her waistband. A huge shot sounded. Andy flew several feet from his chair and when she turned to look she saw his body on the floor with half his head was missing. She turned to the other side. She saw Oscar's feet vanishing from the kitchen into the den. She expected another blast and steadied for it but then she heard voices outside, Jimmy's voice, and Walter saying, "You stay back with that thing, Jimmy. Ain't none of this has to do with you."

And Jimmy said, "You're damn right it does. You're on my goddamn property." There was another blast. It sounded like the one before. She knew it wasn't Jimmy who was shooting Walter. It was Walter shooting. As soon as she heard it she crawled from beneath the table, slipping on Andy's blood. She ran into the den, hearing Walter charging through the kitchen door. She fired blindly into the kitchen, firing at the shoulder she saw for an instant. As she tucked herself into the space between a cabinet and the den doorway, she said, "Walter, why are you doing this shit? I told you I don't know where Max is."

"Bullshit. If that's the case then how come I trailed Jimmy taking Max's truck to a junkyard out near Oxford and saw him pay the guy to crush it all to pieces?"

"I would say you should take that up with Jimmy but I guess it's too late now."

"Screw you, Liz."

There was silence for a moment. Then Liz said, "All right. Max is dead. You're right, Walter. But I didn't kill him. The big wigs from New Orleans did. In fact, he's buried here, on this property. You put your gun down, I'll take you out there to see it."

"He's dead. Why the fuck should I care what you do with the body?"

"Well, if you don't, I don't." She turned from the doorway and aimed at the wall next to the kitchen doorframe behind which he was standing. She hoped the wall would be weak and hollow enough for the bullet to pierce through. But he must've heard her step before she fired. He had already crouched down, was already peering around the corner of the doorframe firing his rifle at her chest. She moved but felt a tearing pain go through the flesh of her shoulder. It took her breath away as absolutely as breeze extinguishing a candle flame. A high ringing sounded in her ears and she looked around and realized she was sitting in the den. Her gun had fallen several feet away. Walter stepped into the room, kicked it even further, all the way to the carpet in the living room. There were sprinkles of blood in his white beard. He aimed the rifle at her head. "Now I'm finally going to do what I've wanted to do since that night you took me and Max out here. You have a real good memory of that night? I sure do. I remember it every time I wash my hands, every time I'm talking to a lady at a bar, every time I jack-off, every time I pick up a fork, every time I open a window."

"Glad to hear you think of me so often."

"I don't think about you. I think about what you've done to me."

She lurched forward and grabbed the barrel and yanked it away from her face and with the arm searing in pain she hit him in the groin. He fell but with one hand still clutching the rifle. She crawled on top of him, placing her hands around his throat. Walter took the bottom of the rifle and smashed it across her mouth and nose and for a few seconds she couldn't see but she could feel the blood dripping from her lips and nostrils. Through the pain she opened her eyes. She grabbed his hand, yanking it from the rifle. She bent her head down and bit into his flesh.

Walter screamed. She bit and bit, bringing her teeth down as hard as she could. His hand tasted of cigarettes and sweat and blood. Though some of the blood, she knew, was her own.

Chapter Twenty

Oscar ran upstairs at the sight of Andy getting shot in the face and darted into a bedroom, where he forced open a window that was hard to budge and climbed over on to the roof of the porch and slid down and landed on his ass and raced to the wall of trees and hedges about a hundred feet away. As he fought through the foliage and thorns he heard more shots. Sweat glazed his limbs, his body felt as if it were humming with a bright yellow light. Soon he was crossing the small and weedy valley he'd seen from the van, his sneakers getting stuck in mud with each step. He climbed up through weeds as high as his waist and stepped on to the gravel road.

"Holy shit," he said, interlacing his fingers and placing them on the back of his head and looking around and listening.

He walked along the edge of the road, listening for gunfire and vehicles. But it was quiet now. He wondered who was alive and who was dead. After ten minutes of walking he came out on to the asphalt road. He looked at his watch and glanced at the sun. It would be at least an hour before sundown. He began running in the direction of Johnson.

By the time he passed the green metal sign saying JOHNSON the mud on his sneakers and the hem on his jeans had dried and huge stars hung over the swaying trees tops. The noise of insects swirled in the air. The diner in town was open. The fluorescent lights inside seemed harsh after coming in from the dark. He sat at a booth, ordered pancakes and scrambled eggs. The waitress barely glanced at him while taking the order. When she left he took a napkin from the dispenser, blew his nose. Then he turned to the three men at the counter. He walked over to them and asked if any of them happened to be going up to Memphis tonight. One said no, the second said yes but in week, and the third said yeah, he had a rig he had to drive north tonight, but he didn't take hitchhikers. Oscar said, "I know it doesn't look like it right now but I'm not some hippie bum trying to thumb a ride. I came down here with some people but they aren't able to take me back up there. And I really need to get back to Memphis tonight."

All three guys looked him over, taking in his swollen cheek and messed up hair and mudcaked shoes, and laughed. "You might not be a hippie bum," said the truck driver, chuckling, "but you sure look like some kind of a bum."

Oscar shook his head, took a step back to his booth. But then he turned again. "You guys ever hear of the Toy Soldiers?"

"Yeah, kind of sounds familiar," said the one who was driving to Memphis in a week.

"I was the lead singer in that band. Listen to this." And he started singing one of their biggest hits, called "Take a Seat in My Plane." The truck driver said yeah, he remembered that song. He was over in Vietnam and him and his buddies used to listen to it on the radio at night. "We loved that song. We'd be way out in the jungle, scared shitless, and we'd hum it under our breath to keep us calm."

The truck driver left him off at his place around two in the morning. The door was closed but unlocked, which was good since he didn't have his keys. After taking a long sudsy bath and putting on clean jeans and a clean polo shirt he called Juanita. No one answered. He called Maria. No answer. He got in his Chevelle and drove down to Cleveland Avenue and parked at Juanita's building. He didn't see her compact blue Volvo but he got out of the car anyway and

136

went through the vestibule and up the steps.

Her door was partly open: a red light shined in the room behind it. As he went up to the door he could hear humming, but it was not Juanita's voice, it was Maria's. She sometimes hummed while in the bath or after making love or while making coffee in the morning. He pressed the door open with his fingertips, stepped into the room on the balls of his feet. Maria stood in the middle of the room in an orange crochet dress, a white silk scarf around her neck. Her hands were at her side. She said, "Are you all right?"

"I've had better nights. What are you doing here?"

"Am I in the wrong place?"

"I didn't know you knew Juanita?"

"I don't."

He approached her. He placed his hands on her bare shoulders. He embraced her. She embraced him back, but feebly, the way an acquaintance might embrace another acquaintance. As he stepped back he rubbed the side of his face, the side that Liz had not struck. "Did Tommy send you?"

"No, but he didn't not send me either."

"You know Tommy well, don't you?"

"We have a deep, tangled history. It's hard to put in words."

"Try me."

She spoke in the hypnotic voice with which she told him her dream some nights ago. "Well, I'm his sister, his lover, his muse, his bitch, his imaginary friend, his beast, his prey, and all of those things work the other way too. What I am to him he is to me."

Oscar began walking around her. She seemed to turn, her face always facing him, without moving her legs or feet. "Your watch, what time does it say?" He gestured toward her wrists.

She held her wrist up. The numerals and hands were there. He glanced at it and glanced at his own and saw they read the same, a few minutes past four-thirty. "Is Liz alive?"

"How would I know?"

"And where's Juanita?"

"That I do know. She's at Frank's place."

"Why would you know about her and not Liz?"

She laughed and the sound of it was oddly reassuring because it reminded him of the way Maria would laugh when he first met her, when she was simply a woman he met at a bar who took a few classes at Memphis State. She went up to him, tugged up the front of his shirt, and placed her hand on his stomach. Her fingers were cold but he didn't move. He kept staring at her face. "Your belly is always so warm," she said. "It warms my hands right up."

He took her hand from his stomach. He kissed her knuckles. He said, "I need to talk to Juanita."

"Just go to Frank's. You'll find her there."

There was a pale blue tint in the eastern sky by the time he arrived at Frank's fieldstone house. Her powder-blue Volvo was parked next to the garage. He knew Frank was still in New York and would not be back for another two weeks. The house was shaped like an L. Juanita's old room, and the room she slept in when staying there, was above the kitchen, which was at the back of the L. He rang the kitchen doorbell over and over again. Finally Juanita answered, standing in a robe and slippers. She said, "I'm guessing it can't be good news if you're here this early in the morning."

At the kitchen table he told her everything about being kidnapped by Liz and the gunfight and the long trek back to Memphis. He did not tell her about Maria since he only half believed in her himself. He opened the bottle of aspirin Juanita had found for him when he came into the house. "The name Diana. Does that name ring any bells?"

She thought, scratching her forearms with her nails. "No. It doesn't. I don't know of anyone named Diana outside of Diana Ross."

"Me neither." Oscar swallowed the tablets with some ice water. He lied, telling her, "It's a name Liz mentioned." Then he said, "I have an idea. Let's go on a road trip for a few days. I think this would be a very good time to get out the hell out of Dodge."

She nodded. "So you really saw a guy get killed today?"

"I watched a guy's head explode, yeah. Every time I so much as blink I see it again."

She kept scratching her forearms, leaving tiny white marks on her skin with the ends of her nails. "You ever feel like you're in a story you somehow got caught up in? That suddenly there's this plot out there we have to follow?"

"Yes, I do. And I imagine we might as well go ahead and follow it." He stood up and said, "I'll go pack. I'll come back in less than an hour."

"You going to be okay going to your place alone?"

"I sure hope so."

When he left the sky had turned pink, the birds chirped in the trees.

Twenty-One

They fought into dusk. They knocked heads and bit into each other and rolled over each other and pummeled each other's side and kicked one another with their knees. Eventually she was able to get her hands around his neck, pinning his hands under her knees. She was exhausted but she sensed he was more exhausted. The intelligence dimmed from his eyes, followed by a mute and dumb awareness. She whispered, "Good bye, Walter," as even that awareness drifted away and all that remained was eye matter.

She stood and immediately fell to her knees. The house around her turned as if it were a cube played with by a child. As she crawled she kept looking at the wound in her shoulder. It was hard keeping her eyes off of it. In the kitchen she pulled at the cord of the phone on the wall and caught the receiver. She got on her knees, reached up, and dialed Horace. "There's a mess here at Jimmy's," she rasped. "Come here quick and bring the doctor with you."

She crawled to the counter and made herself stand. She grabbed the bottle of Jim Beam by the toaster, unscrewed the top. She poured some over the shoulder wound. Tears pressed out through her eyes at the sting of it and she raised the bottle to her lips and drank. She looked down, realizing she'd crawled through Andy's blood to reach the phone. Her legs were covered with it.

Several hours later Horace drove up in his Rabbit with the doctor. She waited for them on the porch, under its spinning ceiling fan and glowing white globe. She had no sense of how long she'd been sitting there. It was as if the night had simply stopped, gathering around her and waiting with her. Minutes and hours were washed away and what remained was the wind fluttering the few leaves she could see in the light of the porch. She heard them approach. Their feet and legs appeared in the porch light before the rest of them did. The doctor suddenly appeared next to her. He checked her eyes and took her pulse and examined the wound on her shoulder and said words to Horace and they helped her up and took her inside and placed her on the couch and a needle slid into her arm and sleep.

When she woke she saw patterns of sunlight on the ceiling, felt breeze on her arms and face. She listened to a woodpecker knock its bill against a tree. She touched her shoulder, letting her fingertips run along the thick bandage. Horace said, "That was a big mess you left for me last night."

"Walter was the one who left it, really."

"I know. I could figure out what went down for the most part. Walter never liked us and the Max thing just pushed him over that last edge."

"My shoulder hurts like fuck."

"Think how much it'd hurt if it'd actually gone in instead of just grazing by."

She turned her head. Horace was in a rocking chair next to the cabinet, resting a cup of coffee on his knee. He wasn't rocking in the slightest. She yawned and looked at the sunlight on the ceiling and said, "This shit with Walter has made me realize we need to clean things up around here. There's something going on I haven't told you about. Something we need to handle." She sat up and started talking about how Oscar and his cousin had been asking questions around Memphis regarding the Edward Parker affair and how she liked Oscar's music and didn't want to see him hurt and had been trying to scare him off his need to find out the truth. She explained how she'd brought him here, hoping to frighten him off the case once and for all. "But Walter fucked it up," she said. "Now Oscar's seen too much. I think instead of scaring him into silence this shit with Walter might send him right into the arms of the police. If he knows I'm alive, he'll know I'm alive because of killing Walter."

Horace leaned forward, placing both hands around his cup of coffee. He'd started to grow a mustache in the past few days and it gave his upper lip a fuzzy look. "You're playing with fire here. Don't you remember what happened to Max? Hell, Liz. Try to think straight. If there's a situation you take care of it. You don't wait around."

"I know. I know. But think of this too. Oscar has a local name. Shit, he used to have a national name. If we beat the shit out of him, it's going to make the news. If we make him disappear, that'd make the news too. There'd be a lot of attention with this guy. Tommy never had that kind of fame so it wasn't the same with him."

"Okay. That's a good point. But I doubt Vince would read it that way." He stood up, pressed his shoulder against the windowsill, and looked out into the yard. "You know what we have to do. Especially now with this guy knowing about this place and the gun fight and all."

"Yeah, I know."

"I detect some sadness in your voice, Liz."

"I really liked this guy. He wrote some really nice songs."

"What do you like better, his songs or your life?"

"Horace, that ain't even a choice." She shifted on the sofa. Her body ached but her shoulder especially hurt. The wound felt like it had been packed with concrete. She asked, "How about getting me one of those cups of coffee? Then I guess it'll be time to get to work."

"I think you should tell me where he lives and some of the people who know him and let me handle it. You might not've noticed but you're in a pretty shitty shape."

"No. I'm all right. And it would feel like letting myself off too easy, letting you handle this guy." Liz looked at the floor of the den and didn't see any blood, though there had been quite a bit the night before. She asked, "And Andy and Jimmy and Walter? What'd you do with them?"

"Like I said, I was busy last night. And early this morning."

"You put Walter near Max?"

"Hell no. That's what Walter would've wanted. I buried Walter way out in that swampy area you see driving in. I did put Andy with Max. They seemed friendly enough the few times I saw them in the same room. And Jimmy I put with his folks out on the west side of the lot. I placed a white stone on it just like the stones he had on his mom and sister."

"The doctor help?"

"Hell yeah. He took off his suit coat and helped. He knows where his bread is buttered."

"He's spry for his age."

"Guys like that never die. They just get replaced by other guys like that." Horace went into the kitchen to make her coffee.

Back at her house she showered, keeping her bandaged shoulder out from the stream of water, and fried three sausages in the skillet. She ate directly from the skillet, using the fork to cut the sausages up. Then she drove down South Parkway to Richard's apartment building. On the small brick shed next to the building someone had spray painted FUCK SUMMER in blocky orange letters. She wondered if one of Richard's punk friends had done it. He let her in, a bandage still on his nose. He wore black jockey shorts and white tube socks and nothing else. "I don't know where he is," he told her.

"He's not going to be at his apartment. I didn't even bother to check. So if he's not at his apartment where would he be?"

Richard threw himself on the sofa and grabbed a pack of cigarettes from the coffee table. "Why do you want to know?"

"You said back in the hospital how it was your policy to

not ask questions and how you thought it best to stay with that policy. I don't see why you should start asking questions now."

He smoked, he rubbed his forehead, he stared blankly at the tabletop. Liz sat beside him and rubbed his lower back and he stiffed but she continued rubbing. "Just give me a few names to go on."

He stared at the table, smoking.

She pressed his shoulders back against the sofa cushions. She took the waistband of his jockey shorts and rolled it down to his knees and took his cock in her hand and played with it. "Three or four names."

"The heroin I gave Tommy, you did something to it." He spoke like a resentful nine-year-old. He pouted his lips. "I've been thinking about that a lot and what it all means."

She didn't say yes or no. She continued stroking his cock. It began to harden. With her other hand she stroked his pale fatless thighs.

He said, "It was tainted which is why you told me not to use any. But what I find striking about it is you know what a selfish asshole I am and that chances were pretty good I would use some. And you didn't care. I could've used it and died and my death would've been on your hands. But you didn't care. You had me deliver the package anyway, knowing what I'm like."

He stared at her, not at her hand. She stared back. His cock was hard and she stroked it fast. He was inhaling from his cigarette as he came. His face barely registered it. There was some trembling of his lips and that was all. She wiped her fingers off on the rough sofa fabric. "Now I've been nice to you so you have to be nice to me."

"I don't have to be shit to you." He pulled his jockey shorts back up.

"Give me some names, Richard."

"No. Not until you admit you almost killed me. Not until you apologize. Not until you beg me for forgiveness."

She brought her hand back and struck him in the center of

his stomach and he curled into a ball and edged up into the corner of the sofa.

She grabbed the hands he had over his face, pulling them away. "Come on," she said. "Let me see your face."

He continued to fight her but she was stronger even with her wounded shoulder and she peeled his arms back away from him and looked into his face. He wasn't crying. His eyes, though, appeared empty of everything but hate and fear. When she let go of his arms she crossed the room and left the apartment, knowing she would never return there again. He had drifted past her. He would never open himself out to her again.

She drove down Jackson Avenue, to North Evergreen Street. She parked in front of a two-story house with a weedy yard where a woman in jean shorts was bathing a small boy in a metal bucket on the porch. In the driveway a shirtless man worked on a Volkswagen van, his arms smeared with oil. Liz nodded to the man as she passed and to the woman on the porch as she stepped into the house.   She found George eating a hamburger and examining the charcoal sketches he had on the drawing table in front of him of dragons and hippie princes on full-bodied unicorns and long hair princess with roses in their lush pubic hair poised on stoic bullfrogs. He had his back to the doorway, didn't turn around as she neared him. "George, why did you not destroy the negatives?"

He looked at her, still chewing. When he swallowed, he said, "You mean the ones with that dude from the City Council?"

She nodded.

George peered at her through his thick, smudged glasses. "How did you find out?"

"Some guys in New Orleans know some guys in New York."

"Jesus. Ya'll are worse than the FBI and CIA put together. You have every house in America bugged?"

"Don't give me that hippie paranoid bullshit. Just tell me."

"What're you going to do with me if I don't? This house is filled with people. I don't know how many are here right now but I know if I scream somebody is going to hear me."

Liz took the hamburger from his fingers and squeezed it in her hand, throwing in on the floor. "You think a single one of them is going to rush up here to help you? Most of them saw me coming in. They know what I look like and I bet you've even told a few of them what I do."

On the metal stool next to the drawing board set a glass ashtray and she noticed one of his hands reach behind his back for it. She grabbed the back of his neck, twisting him to the ground. His glasses fell from his ears as he took hold of her wrist and struggled to remove her grip. She squeezed the way she'd squeezed the burger. "Don't you dare yell, you hear?"

He choked out a few syllables. She threw him face first toward the floor. When he sat up on his knees, rubbing the back of his neck, he told her, "It was your little buddy."

"I have a lot of them."

"The real short blond dude. Horace. He told me not to tell you or anybody else."

She stared at him. She heard the mother outside on the porch, cooing to her child. Finally she said, "You're lying."

"Liz, I'm telling you the truth." He crouched on the balls of his feet. "If I stand up, is it going to be okay? We won't whack me on the side of the head or anything?"

"Stand up. I won't hurt you."

As he rose up he dusted off the back of his jeans. "You must've really fucked up your arm to have a bandage like that."

"It's none of your goddamn business. Now explain yourself."

"Horace came by one night back in January and said he thought he could get a good price on the pictures. He said there weren't too many photos out there of old white guys doing what he was doing with Diana and certain printers of certain types of books would take an interest."

146

"He knew he wasn't supposed to do it."

"That's right. Which is why he told me to tell anybody who might ask about it that it was Randy's doing, not his."

"And why aren't you telling me that now? How come you're not pinning it on Randy?"

"For one thing, I like Randy better than I like Horace. For another, I'm leaving Memphis tonight to go out someplace where I'm sure you assholes can't find me. Not because I'm running but because I'm a traveling man. I don't like sticking to one place too long. And thirdly, I think what white people have done to black people for who knows how long is pretty shitty and Horace's plan to lay it on the black dude never sat right with me." He picked up his glasses from the floor, gingerly placed them back on. "So what are you going to do?"

"I'll talk to Horace about it. That's all I can do."

"No. I mean about me. Are you going to beat the shit out of me for ratting out Horace?"

She nodded no and slowly walked out. As she reached the porch she paused, looking at the woman with her sunburnt face and breasts and belly. "Could I ask you to do me this huge favor? I'll make it worth your while. I'm trying to find a friend, this guy who owes me money, and I know his buddies aren't going tell me where he's at if I ask, but I don't think they'd have a problem if a pretty woman they never met before was asking about him." She reached into her back pocket and pulled out her sheath of twenties and started counting them out and placing them next to the ice cream.

Part Three: Warszawa

June 1978

Twenty-Two

Oscar and Juanita were perched on two orange-fringed pillows watching one woman give another a tattoo. They were in the Chelsea Hotel and it was nearing midnight. The woman was named Valerie. She wore a huge fox fur over her shoulders and there was a tattoo of a thin, curled mustache over her mouth that Frank had told him she'd done herself. The woman getting the tattoo had flat black hair with a patch of purple feathers tied into it, above her ear. Oscar had heard she was a musician and a poet and had recently returned from Paris, where's she'd almost starved to death. "It's going to be beautiful," the musician said to Valerie. It was of a black thunderbolt. The musician glanced up at him and Juanita. "Don't you think it's going to be beautiful?"

"It's pretty," said Oscar. He'd been drinking since two in the afternoon.

"It's more than pretty," Valerie told him. "It's a thunderbolt."

There was a knock on the door and Frank stepped in wearing a tan suit and an open collared shirt. He nodded to everyone, turned to Juanita and Oscar. "The guy in my usual room isn't leaving until Monday, so I'll be staying with Violet tonight. They have a room on the junkies' floor if you dare to stay there."

"Does it have a door with a lock?" asked Oscar.

"It does, though I'm not sure it'll do you much good."

"Come on, Frank," said the musician. "Junkie can't harm

you. All they do is stare at the walls waiting for the next fix."

Valerie turned, looking at Frank over the fox fur. "That Sex Pistol still up there with his girl?"

"Far as anyone knows," said Frank. He was fixing a drink from the bottles of rum and whiskey and seltzer water and Coke on the table between the windows. "Nobody has seen them for days but that's not unusual. I think when they die up there nobody will know about it for weeks. The stench will be the only thing giving it away."

"The Sex Pistols don't exist anymore," the musician said.

"I saw them in Memphis," Oscar told her. "Even then they were barely staying together. There wasn't anything keeping them together but noise and spittle and nasty thoughts."

"Those things keep a lot of things together these days," said the musician, toying with the feathers in her hair.

"Frank, don't be so hard on those two love birds up there," Valerie told him, focusing back on the tattoo. "They're a young couple in love. I saw them screwing each other in the elevator one night."

"In my day we courted by taking river boats along the Mississippi," Frank said, stirring his drink with a fork. "We would wear straw hats and someone on board always knew how to play the accordion. It would be hot as blazes but the ice in our drinks never melted."

"And no fucking I presume," said the musician.

"No, there would be fucking," Frank said, sipping his drink. "We didn't call it that though. We called it grazing. The boat would pull up to a dock every few hours and the couples would walk up into the weeds and hedges nearby and graze until the steam whistle sounded. Then we would dry ourselves with handkerchiefs and button whatever had been unbuttoned and return to the boat, where our drinks would be waiting for us exactly where we left them."

Valerie rubbed blood from the musician's knee with a damp rag and sat back on the sofa, saying she needed to take a break. Juanita told Frank, "Dad, tell them the room is fine. I don't mind."

"I'm surprised this place is so crowded," Oscar said. "It's so big you'd think there would always be an extra few rooms."

"This place is full of ghosts," said Frank, "who make it impossible to tell how many rooms are actually taken." He sipped his drink again. "Juanita, how about this? You to stay with Violet and I'll take it upon myself to venture with Oscar into the junkies' den."

"Dad, you're being ridiculous. It's just for two nights anyway. You said yourself you'd have your usual room back by Monday."

"Have you ever been on that floor?" Frank asked her.

"No, but I bet you haven't either."

Frank told her, "I don't have to. I've heard enough stories about what goes on up there to not have to see it for myself."

Valerie said, "Frank, you need to let your little girl grow up."

He smiled at her. "Valerie, I love you until the cows come home, but you really need to keep out of this."

She flipped him the middle finger. "You're a real southern gentleman sometimes, asshole."

Oscar said, "We could stay someplace else. It's not like this is the only hotel in town."

Frank moved toward the door, stirring his drink again. "Many of those places are worse than here." He turned to Juanita and Oscar. "Juanita, go ahead and try it out tonight but we'll switch if there are any problems. Oscar, if anything should happen to her, I'll get one of my guns and blow your goddamn head off. Be forewarned." He turned to the musician. "Was Paris good?"

"I almost died there."

He opened the door, his drink still in hand. "Glad to hear you had a good time. Good night, everyone."

After he left, Valerie looked over at Juanita. "What is it like having him for a father?" She rubbed the musician's knee with the rag again.

"Confusing," said Juanita.

Around two Oscar walked to the elevators. One was broken and the when the other opened he smelled piss inside. He took the dim stairs several floors down, passing a skinny tabby cat near the first floor. He got the key from the heavyset man behind the desk who wore a shabby red suit and trudged back up the staircase. On the junkies' floor no one was around. Oscar and Juanita walked quickly down the corridor, and he unlocked their door. The room was clean and spare and one of the windows had been left open and you could hear light traffic moving down West 23rd Street. There was a lamp in the corner. When Juanita turned it on they found a pencil drawing a former resident had left on the wall. It showed Elvis crucified on a cross, blood pouring from his hands and feet and side. At the top of the cross the drawing showed a scroll of paper that read ELVIS HAS LEFT THE BUILDING instead of ECCE HOMO. "A little bit of home," said Juanita.

The following morning Oscar and Juanita and Frank and Violet ate breakfast at a diner a few blocks north of the Chelsea. Violet was saying, "Tonight we're going to a jazz concert at a loft on Bond Street. You two are welcome to join us. It promises to be very noisy and atonal."

"These two prefer rock and roll," said Frank. "For them music started around late fifty-three, early fifty-four."

"Dad thinks we're the barbarians invading Rome," Juanita told Violet. "Not just Oscar and I but everyone under the age of forty."

"I'm under forty," Violet said to Frank.

"You have no age, dear," he replied. "You're like the Mona Lisa. Empires will rise and fall but you keep moving through the ever-burning landscape."

"Frank likes to pretend he worships me from afar," she said to Juanita and Oscar. "He likes to pretend he's never fucked me."

Frank poured sugar into his coffee. "I beg to differ with that implication. The act of love only increases the mystery."

"I don't really think I want to hear this conversation," said Juanita.

Frank looked up from the mug. "I'm sure Mother is with some garden boy even as we speak."

"Yeah, that's enough," she told him.

Violet touched Oscar's wrist. "You've been pretty quiet this morning. Something on your mind?"

He glanced at Juanita and then at Frank and then at Violet and said, "I've had a rough few weeks."

Frank told her, "He showed up at my house a while back all beat up, looking like a canary that'd been half-eaten by a cat."

"Poor baby," Violet said, squeezing his wrist again.

Frank took some cash from his billfold and counted out a few fives and placed them in the center of the table. He said, "Violet and I have to head out. There's a show at the Met we're going to check out."

"Let's walk part of the way, Frank," Violet suggested. "We can get a cab when we start to get tired."

"We'll get our shoes dirty."

"Don't you have another pair at the hotel?"

"Yes," he said. "I have many pairs." He shrugged. "Let's walk then."

After they left, Oscar and Juanita both lit cigarettes. They stared out the window at the passing cars. A teenager with an enormous Afro handed out prayer cards on the corner, a rosary hanging from his neck. "Black Jesus is coming!" he yelled at the passerby. "Black Jesus is here! You won't find him on TV! You won't find him up there in heaven! He's here, right now! He's among you when you least expect it, motherfuckers!"

Juanita said, "I don't know when we'll be able to go back."

"It's crossed my mind that maybe we should move here. Your dad lives here more than half the time anyway."

"I don't want to live here. All my friends are in Memphis. Mom is in Memphis. New York is just a place I visit."

"You don't have a boyfriend right now."

"So what? That doesn't mean I want to leave my life down there behind."

"We're really bad detectives, aren't we?"

"The worst."

Juanita said she wanted to walk around Central Park, maybe go to the zoo. She needed fresh air to take her mind off the situation at hand. Oscar told her he was tired, having not slept well last night. He'd meet up with her later in the day but he wanted to take a nap right now.

Back at the hotel he could hear coughing behind one door and a man speaking with his mother behind another. The man kept saying, "Yes, Mother. That is correct Mother. I will be in Virginia during those dates and possibly a few days earlier."

In his room he took off his clothes and washed his face and under his arms and behind his neck. The cold water refreshed him. In bed he stared across the room at the drawing of the crucified Elvis. He thought about adding something to it. After several minutes he decided no, it was complete as it was. As soon as he placed his head on the pillow he heard feet and hands crawling through the open window. He bolted up, thinking a junkie had found a way to break into the room. But it was Maria standing in the window, the gauze curtain breathing behind her in the summer breeze. "I've never been this far north before," she said. She wore the same crochet dress as before. Her hair was a mess and there were streaks of dried mud in it. She sat on her knees at the end of his bed, placed his feet in her lap, and started stroking his ankles. "Though I take that back. Tommy took me here once. We visited the tigers and fed them meat. Tommy fed them from his mouth. He'd put a strip of bacon between his teeth and one of the lions would come up and lick it from his face."

"This doesn't seem likely."

"I might be exaggerating a little."

"Tommy's dead. And I have no idea who you are."

"I've told you. I take classes at Memphis State. I want to

be a social worker." She rubbed his calves. "You're tense."

"Who's Tommy?"

"He's a friend of yours, now dead. What an odd thing to ask."

Oscar gently pulled his legs away and walked over to the window and glanced out at the perfect sky, a single plane silently crossing it, drifting east toward the ocean. "Last time we talked you said you were his sister, his lover, all sorts of shit. Can't you narrow it down?"

"We were going to be twins but a convergence happened in the womb and we became one and more than one."

"So somehow you really are his sister?"

"No, we never existed apart long enough for that. A better way to think of it is that I was the girl he'd met by the pond some summers. But I was dead before I met him and I'll be dead long after."

"How did you die?"

"I have a vague memory of stones and being buried by a pond. But Tommy claims to have the same memories. So they might be symbolic more than literal."

"Did Tommy ever throw a stone at you?"

Maria stood up off the bed and walked over to him. "You should hear yourself talk. You know Tommy. He could never hurt anyone."

"Except this guy Edward Parker."

"He didn't have much choice. Liz was giving him drugs for free. Or for what he thought was free. But then she asked a favor. And at first he said no. But she said then he had to pay her what he owed. And of course he didn't have it. And she said it would only be a few pictures anyway, what did he care. And she told him this Edward Parker was a jerk who mistreated his mistress by promising her more clothes and a better apartment and a new car but never delivering on those promises and not even sending her a card or a note when her mother died. Anyway, that's what I've heard. That's one of the rumors swirling around."

Maria crawled out the window on to the balcony. Oscar

followed her out, standing next to her at the floral wrought-iron railing. She gazed at him. "You're naked, you know."

"And I don't know what you are."

She pinched his ear, hard. "Listen to the walls, find Diana, and keep your head low and you'll come out of this and one piece."

She crawled over the wrought-iron railing and clung to its side. As she let go she blew him a kiss. He turned as she drifted down. He went inside and closed the window and jumped on the mattress, tugging the sheet up over his head.

He had no notion of the time when he awoke. His chest was glazed with sweat, he felt chilled and feverish. In the bathroom he looked in the mirror and noticed his cheeks were flushed. He brushed his teeth and dressed in the clothes he'd worn earlier that day. At the desk downstairs one of the clerks called him over. He had a pencil mustache over his mouth and long shiny fingernails. "Are you Oscar of room 319?"

"That would be me."

"I have a message for you. We tried your phone but it might not be working." He handed Oscar a piece of paper. It read CALL BRIAN and it gave Brian's home number.

"Can I call here?" Oscar asked.

"Can you pay for long distance?"

"My uncle can. His name's Frank."

"I know Frank. He's a generous man. Yes, use our phone."

There were three phones behind the desk, each one black. Oscar picked up the receiver of one and dialed. Brian said, "New York treating you good?"

"Good enough. This is pretty expensive, Brian. What can I do you for?"

"This real pretty lady came by the studio earlier asking about you. She said you and her went out a while back and she was trying to get a-hold of you."

"Tell here I'll be back when I get back. This stay is a little indefinite, okay man? If she really needs me for something urgent, give her the number here." Oscar shivered. He wondered how high his fever was.

"Well, I told her where you were, in New York at the Chelsea." He paused. He added, "But when she left, something about her didn't set right, so I looked out the office window and saw her climbing into this big van this fat woman was sitting in. She had on this black vest and a gray hat with a black brim exactly like the one Brando wears in The Wild One. You know this chick?"

Oscar laughed. He shivered and he laughed and he rubbed the bridge of his nose. "Oh, man, Brian, it's all right. Don't worry about it, okay?"

"Worry about what?"

"Nothing, Brian. I know her. It's nothing to worry about."

"You in trouble?"

"You know me. I'm always in a little bit of trouble. I'll see you around, you hear?" He hung up and thanked the clerk. Then he asked if he happened to have any aspirin. The clerk shook his head but said there was a grocery not far from there that would. Oscar stepped out under the red awning. He lit a cigarette, then turned in the direction of Central Park, walking slowly up 5th Avenue. He knew it would be a long trek but he didn't care. He wanted to be in the open, around people, with as many eyes on him as possible.

Twenty-three

She called Horace, told them they were going to New York.
"I don't know if I can just drop my shit and go," he said.

"I can't drive up there alone with my arm the way it is,"
she told him. "And I'm sure as shit not taking the bus or
plane with the stuff I'm going to be carrying with me."

"Could you give me an hour to settle some things and
pack?"

"In an hour, then." She hung up the phone in the den and
took the suitcase from the closet and threw in some shirts
and jeans. From the kitchen she took a screwdriver and
carried it into the bedroom and pried up three floorboards
near her bed. Beneath the floorboards sat a towel. She
picked up the towel, placing it on the mattress, as if a live
creature napped inside its folds. She pulled back the edges of
the towel and glanced at the pistol and shotgun. They had
been bought from a guy in Natchez with a patchy beard and
a Cajun accent. There were other weapons under other
floorboards but she thought this would be all she needed for
this trip.

After she packed the van, throwing in a bag of bread and
Coke and chips, she removed her map from under the seat
and drew a thick red line across the path they would need to
travel, a big arc moving north from I-40 to I-81 to I-78, and
on in through the Holland Tunnel.

Horace stood on the sidewalk in front of his house,
waiting for her. Two suitcases were at his feet. "I can drive

for a while," he said after he climbed in.

"No, I'm good for now. You sleep and when my arm starts getting to me I'll give you a shake."

"How long is this going to be?"

"To get there? About eighteen hours, depending on traffic. Once we get there, I don't figure it's going take too long. There's not much to talk over with him at this point."

"And the girl?"

"I think we should leave her alone."

"I'm not so sure, Liz. I think it's highly likely he's told her everything. We should ask ourselves how Vince would handle this."

She glanced over at him. "We'll think about it."

About an hour outside of Nashville she pulled over, shook Horace awake. "My arm is just about to give out on me," she said.

After they switched she took out her box of Seconal from the glove department. She swallowed one with some Coke she'd poured into a Styrofoam cup. "Those red devils?" Horace asked.

"The reddest and the devilest."

"That's some deadly shit there. Jimi Hendrix died from it. Marilyn Monroe. Judy Garland. Or at least they all had that shit in their bloodstream."

"You sound like a message brought to you by an anti-drug campaign."

"I'm just saying those things aren't as innocent as they might look."

"They look like bullets of blood. I don't think they look innocent at all."

When she woke up they had reached the outer edge of Knoxville and the sky in the east had lightened. "Eleven hours to go," said Horace.

"Eleven if we're lucky."

For lunch they pulled into a small Virginia town called Marketsville, found a diner next to a Shell gas station. The windows of the diner were so clean the glass seemed invisible. From her seat Liz could see a sandwich board sign someone had placed in front of the Shell Station. It read BLAME JIMMY CARTER FOR THIS. Liz said to Horace, "I know about the photographs."

Horace glanced up. "You're going have to be more specific."

"No, I don't think I have to be."

They continued eating in silence and when the waitress came with their bill they split it, paying their own. At the van Liz walked around to the back and asked Horace for some help moving something. As he went up to her she grabbed the hair at the back of his head and shook him and said, "What the fuck were you thinking? You're not a dumb guy, Horace." She threw him against the van. When he lunged at her she caught him by the shoulders and threw him again against the van, as if he were a straw puppet. This time he struck the side of his head against it and collapsed on to the sidewalk holding his scalp. "Fuck you, Liz," he muttered. "Don't you ever do that to me again."

Liz turned and looked at the elderly couple staring at her and Horace. Liz said, "Mind your own goddamn business. This doesn't concern you."

The man placed his arm over his wife's shoulder. They swiftly walked away toward the diner, not even glancing over their shoulders.

Horace said, "I did it before the thing that happened to Max. I really would've been stupid to do that afterwards."

"Why didn't you tell me?"

"You never skimmed a little off the side? I didn't think it was a big deal. There's a guy in Chicago I know who has a cousin in New York who prints those books in the basement of his apartment building. I mentioned I had these photographs he might be interested in. That's how it started."

"How much you get paid?"

"You want in on it?"

"No I don't. I'm just curious."

"A few hundred." As he stood up he continued to hold the side of his head. With his free hand he picked up his sunglasses, placed them back on.

"So you risked your life for a few hundred dollars? Goddamn you, Horace."

"It was before what Vince did Max. Liz, I keep telling you this."

"What are we going to do? Vince was the one to put me on the case. He found out about the pictures circulating out there."

"Why did he talk to you and not me?"

"I imagine he likes me better."

He laughed. "You know, you can all go fuck yourselves."

"You told George to blame it on Randy."

"Yeah, I did, and we can still do that."

"No we can't."

"Because you like Randy."

"Because I like Randy."

"It's not like Vince is going to execute the accused here. I think you're overestimating the nature of the problem. He'll send in some guys to make some noise and rough somebody up but that'll be the extent of it."

"Think back on that afternoon with Max. You really so sure I'm overestimating?" She gestured toward the van. "We need to get back on the road. We'll figure this out later."

Liz drove the van to the Shell station and Horace pumped more gas in the tank and then they were moving north again on I-81. The air-conditioner blew out lukewarm air. Horace fiddled with different knobs on it but the air never turned cooler. They rolled down their windows. Their faces were glossy with sweat. Liz said, "I used to live out here, in Virginia. After I moved from Little Rock I lived over there in Roanoke. I was seventeen. I ran away from home with this guy from school. He was the only guy I knew fat as I was. He was interesting, though. He grew his hair long before any of the other kids did and he was the first one I knew who got his hands on some weed."

"Sounds like a good guy."

"The night before we were going away, his older brother let me borrow his gun. They were all a bunch of rednecks. The boy, his brother, his parents, so for them letting somebody borrow a gun wasn't any different than letting somebody borrow a cup of sugar. The boy I was with, he was going out into the woods with his daddy's rifle at the age of eleven."

They were drifting down the side of a mountain, an enormous valley to their east. "What did you need with the gun?" Horace asked, opening a tube of Pringles.

"It was for mama. Over the years she just got worse and worse. When I was a kid I used to feel sorry for her but that was long gone by then. She'd wake up drunk and go to bed drunk and the guys she'd bring over just got meaner and meaner. Sometimes when mama was taking a shower and they'd run into me somewhere around the house they tried to get with me, you know? They'd come up and rub my back and whisper in my ear. But I'd tell them to get the fuck away and they must've known I was serious because they always did."

"Is that why you got so big?"

"What?"

"Is that why you got so big? To keep the guys off you? To make yourself less of an attractive option to the male eye?"

"You're an asshole, Horace. I'm fat because I eat a lot. And I eat a lot because I like food."

He offered her the tube of chips. She shook her head no.

"Go on," he said. "You've never told me this one before."

"Well, this last night, the night before I ran away from Little Rock with this boy, I heard mama and some dude in her room really going at it. I heard those sounds every night of the week so it wasn't anything new. But that night I had the gun, this little snub-nosed thing. I opened the door, stepped inside. Mama was on all fours with her dressed hitched up all the way to her shoulders and this hairy guy with part of his ear missing was fucking her from behind.

They both turned and stared at me and he kept fucking her and mama kept moaning and it was like I could've been a cat or a cockroach coming into the room, nothing more. Sure not somebody's daughter. Only when I took the gun out and aimed it at them did they move." She laughed and glanced over at Horace. "You would've liked it, Horace. It was your kind of thing. They both crouched down on the other side of the bed and mama was sobbing and the guy was just pleading with me, telling me I could take his truck, I could do whatever, just let him live."

"That does sound funny," Horace said, eating another chip. "I would've liked to see that shit."

"I stood there for a good thirty seconds, really eating it up. Then I raised the gun and fired three times at the ceiling. Then I walked out the front door and the boy was waiting for me in his truck at the curb. And we sped right out of Little Rock. And I never saw her again."

"Really? How many years ago was that?"

Liz stuck her elbow out the opened window and dabbed the back of her sweaty neck with a bandanna. "It was the mid-sixties. A long time ago."

"She alive?"

"No. She passed on. My aunt called me, telling me about it. It was the winter of seventy-one. Mama died from a heart attack behind some bar. She was thirty-eight years old."

"You think you'll make it to thirty-eight?"

"Yep. Or I'll die trying."

Twenty-Four

Oscar found Juanita sitting on a bench in the Primates House, an orange scarf with a green floral pattern covering her hair. The smell and humidity and heat in the building pressed against his face and he covered his nose with a handkerchief. He sat beside her and said, "I have some not so great news."

"Just once I'd like to see you and have you say something different."

"Liz knows we're here in New York. Brian told her. He didn't know what he was doing. After he did it he felt uneasy about it so he called the hotel."

"He doesn't know Liz, right?"

"Not at all. He doesn't know about any of this stuff. But Liz sticks out from the crowd. He saw her in her Marlon Brando get-up and thought it might be a good idea to keep me informed."

A monkey jumped up on the bars of its cage and wailed its monkey song. A group of young girls, some carrying heart-shaped helium balloons, made the noise back at it. Every sound in the building echoed. Oscar stared up at the ceiling with its cracked plaster and saw a pigeon flying around. Juanita asked, "Are you sick? Just sitting next to you, you seem to be generating this warmth."

"It's probably my usual sunny self you're feeling."

She touched her hand against his forehead. Her palm felt cool and dry. "You need to rest. You shouldn't go to that party tonight on Bond Street."

"You're right. I should wait around at the hotel for Liz."

She looked at Oscar, smiling bitterly and ironically. "What the hell are we going to do, Oscar? Should we go to the police? I think it might be time."

"Well, you don't have anything to worry about. She's never shown any interest in you. She never followed you and she never kidnapped you. She wants to talk to me." He coughed into the handkerchief, wiped his nose. "I've been thinking about this. She likes me. As fucked up as it sounds, I know she's protecting me. At the end of the day she wants absolute assurance on my part that I'm done asking questions about Tommy. And that I'm not going to discuss with the cops what happened out there in Choctaw County. If we call the police we fuck it up. I have no idea how many people she's connected to but I imagine if she does wind up going to jail her friends aren't going take too kindly to it."

"You really have been thinking about this."

"Of course, I could be totally wrong, and maybe she's coming up here to kill me. But I don't think so. I'd feel more scared if that was the case."

They took a cab down 5th Avenue to West 14th Street. Once on Broadway Oscar saw a figure in a denim shirt with curly hair and a familiar gait. He peered out the window, his palms drenched with sweat. He hurriedly edged forward. "Mister, could you let me out here, at the curb?" he called out.

Juanita said, "What are you doing?"

"I'll meet you at Bond Street in an hour." He glanced at the back of the retreating figure that looked like Maria. She was going past a trashcan that had been spilled over, spewing cans and bags and cartons over the sidewalk. As he closed the door behind himself he heard the door on the other side open and shut. He turned, saw the taxi drive away. Juanita stood on the sidewalk. "You have a fever of more than one hundred, I bet, and you have a violent woman after you. I'm not going to let you walk around alone."

"It's that woman up there. I think you know her."

"A former lost love?"

"I don't know if I'd put it that way. We've had some interesting experiences together, I'll say that."

They crossed the street, walking fast. Maria was about a block away, if it was Maria. Oscar stared to walk faster: he out-paced Juanita. Juanita told him, "I think your fever is messing with your head."

"You were the one who decided to follow me."

They passed a green metal door with two stone steps in front of it. The steps were covered with bird shit. Oscar stopped, approached a poster next to the door. It showed a black woman in spotlight wearing a sequined wrap dress. Her huge head of hair was parted in the middle. A ring of blue mascara circled each eye. Beneath the image were the letters DIANA. The poster must've been hanging for some time because the upper corner had peeled off and the colors had a sunfaded quality. Oscar approached it and looked into the face of the poster and said, "This is it." Then he lost all strength, crashing downward.

He felt hands around him and he felt his body being taken somewhere, dragged. Two men were placing him on a couch. Juanita hovered over him, looking worried. There was a filing cabinet in the room and a desk with a green-shaded lamp. One of the men had a small Afro and wore a red scarf around his neck. The other man was older, with gray flecks in his busy beard and hair, and he was dressed in a maroon corduroy jacket and pants. The older man said, "Good thing me and Otis were coming up the sidewalk. You could've really busted your head with that fall if Otis here didn't grab you."

"I have a bad cold."

"I figured something was up."

Otis nodded to the older man and left the office. The older man introduced himself as Samuel. Juanita said, "Thank you for your help, Samuel."

"Yeah," Oscar said, sitting up. "Thanks. I got kind of dizzy

166

out there. I took a long walk earlier and think I exhausted the few resources I had."

"Sit back, okay? Just sit for a few minutes. No use getting up and walking out the door and having you collapse all over again."

Oscar thanked him and introduced himself and then Juanita stepped forward with her hand out and introduced herself. The room was cool. An air-conditioner roared in the window. "Samuel, what's the name of your palace?" asked Oscar.

"I know it's narcissistic but I named it after myself. I consider it my home. I even sleep here. I have a little room upstairs with a sink and bathtub. So when people enter 'Samuel's' they really are. This really is my place." Samuel went up to a curtain and pulled it back to reveal a bar and tables and three brass chandeliers. No one was in it. "Four hours from now it'll be hopping. We don't bother to open the doors until ten. We used to open them earlier but all we got was a bunch of sad old drunks who'd dampen the mood of the place, if you know what I mean." He pulled the curtain back, removed a cigar from the pocket of his jacket. "We welcome all types: white and black and queer and non-queer. This is my place and I welcome everyone."

Oscar was shivering so much his back teeth were chattering and his hands and face felt like bricks that had been baked by the sun for hours. He said, "And who is Diana? She sing here? She looks a lot like Diana Ross."

"She does, doesn't she? She has one thing Lady Diana will never have though. Two things actually, though only one you might've noticed in the poster."

Juanita said, "You make her sound like the riddle of the Sphinx."

Samuel smiled, breathing smoke out toward the ceiling. "You give up? A penis and an Adam's apple."

Oscar looked at his hands, trying hard to concentrate. "Where is she from?"

"Women like her often have to fixed abode. She's from

Mississippi just like I was once upon a time. She moved back and forth between here and Memphis for a few years. Last I heard she's on the Lower East Side. She hasn't sung here in quite some time though I keep the poster up because she had a devoted fan base. I like to have them wander in every so often asking about her."

"We're from Memphis too," Juanita said, smiling at Samuel and sitting next to Oscar.

"Everyone from down there has to pass through Memphis at some point in their lives, it seems like."

Oscar asked, "You happen to have her address?"

"You a fan?" asked Samuel.

Juanita stared at him. "Oscar, why are you asking about that?"

"Tommy knew her." He said to Samuel, "I don't know her but a close friend of mine did. He's dead now but he told me to tell her something if I should ever run across her."

"I could maybe relay the message, should I ever cross paths with her again."

"It's sort of personal. He told it to me shortly before he died." Samuel puffed on his cigar. He placed it in the swan-shaped ashtray on his desk and half-sat on the edge of the desk and answered, "It's a policy of mine never to hand out addresses of people who've worked for me, or who might work for me in the future. But you seem like a nice enough guy, so I'll tell you this. There's this delicatessen where she hangs out when she's in town. She lives nearby. If she's in town you'll be sure to run into her if you drop by there two or three nights in a row. It's her nocturnal hangout spot. It's a real rough place, though, just to let you know. That whole area of town is as bad as the Bronx. I ain't kidding. I might go down Houston Street to meet a friend but if it's night I don't go any further south than that."

Oscar stood, wiping his damp palms on his jeans. "You've been a big help, Samuel. Maybe we'll drop by sometime later tonight."

"You two would be more than welcome to drop by. If you

do, tell Jerry, the bartender here, that I said you could have a round of drinks on the house. All right?" He shook their hands, led them back out into the street.

As soon as the door closed Oscar began explaining. "Here's why Edward Parker killed himself. The woman he was seeing wasn't a woman entirely. He was seeing Diana. So the pictures Liz had Tommy take weren't of him with a black woman. That would've caused a scandal and but it would've blown over. No, I'm guessing the pictures were of him in bed with a black guy who looks like Diana Ross. That's what he couldn't deal with at the end of the day. He couldn't live knowing there were photographs of him with Diana floating out there."

They were walking west. They passed a group of Latino men playing checkers on the sidewalk next to a small grocery store. Juanita said, "That does make a lot more sense. But don't you think it was a huge coincidence that you happened to see that poster? There are thousands of old posters hanging around."

"I think I was being led there."

"By this mystery woman you saw from the taxi?"

"Why not?"

"Your fever must be dangerously high, Oscar. You better not die on me tonight. I'll be severely disappointed."

"I'm going to try my best."

The sun had started to set while they were in Samuel's office and only the tops of the buildings on the east side of the street were lit with daylight. The street itself stood already in dusk. Juanita hailed a cab and told the driver to drive them to Bond Street.   In the cab she said, "But why do you want to talk to her? Or to him? To Diana, I mean. I think we have a pretty good picture of what happened now."

"We've already come this far. Don't you want to meet the woman who started it all?"

"Meeting her won't bring Tommy back."

Oscar sneezed into his handkerchief. He wiped his nose

and tucked his hands under his armpits and shivered. "I know that. I know."

The taxi pulled up to the address: a tall building flanked by two smaller ones with a fire escape crisscrossing along its façade. As Juanita paid the driver Oscar watched a woman in a massive fur coat appear near the top of the fire escape. The coat was unbuttoned and she wore a one-piece bathing suit beneath it. Oscar wished he had that coat. It looked warm and he imagined himself snuggling with it in bed. They stepped on the sidewalk. Sirens wailed down the street. Juanita said, "Dad told me what they play here is not so much music as intellectual demonstrations of what music might one day be."

"I'm so out of it I think I'd enjoy just about anything equally."

They went up a narrow staircase that smelled of pot and perfume. A man in a white halter-top stood at the door on the second floor with a shoebox that had the word DONATIONS written on its side. Juanita placed a roll of bills in it, nodding to the man. He nodded back, not smiling but not looking unfriendly either. Just disinterested. He did not know them and they did not know him.

Twenty-Five

Liz asked the man behind the desk, "Could I please know the room number for a man by the name of Oscar Hilton?"

The man lowered the newspaper, slid a large ledger book at his elbow over to where he could read it. "Let me see here," he told her. He looked like he was in his eighties. His hands trembled as his finger went down the names. Most of his fingernails were blackened and chipped. "Are you sure that's the name he checked in here with?"

"I guess he could've used a fake one."

"Oh, wait. I apologize. Here it is." He told her the third room on the fourth floor. Liz thanked him and she and Horace walked to the bank of elevators. One opened and a man who looked like Richard walked out, wearing a cheetah-print T-shirt. She and Horace went to the fourth floor and found the door. Horace carried a satchel over his shoulder and she carried several pistols and switchblades in the interior pockets of her leather jacket. The door was partly open. Liz tapped it further open with the tip of her boot. She walked in, hearing music, a ragtime piano piece. She saw a lean man with graying hair sitting at a small piano in the corner. She listened, the title coming to her, "Maple Leaf Rag." Her aunt had a record of ragtime tunes she would play when she had her and her mother over for dinner. The man spoke. "Is that you, Violet? Doesn't sound like you."

"Where's Oscar? We were told this is his room."

"Who told you such a thing?" His fingers continued

moving across the keyboard. He still had not looked over his shoulder at them.

"The guy downstairs," said Horace. "The clerk." His voice was rough and aggressive. "Where is he?"

The man still played. Then he stopped in mid-song and turned and took a cigarette from his pocket and lit it. "There has been a terrible mistake, I'm afraid. This happens now and then."

"What?" She gripped the switchblade in her pocket.

"The record keeping system in this hotel is not of a very high quality. Here is what probably occurred. My nephew, whose first name is Oscar, came here asking for which room I was in. Whoever gave him that room number probably then asked Oscar if he wanted a room. He probably said he did but he wanted to check with me first, thinking he could sleep on my floor if there was space. The clerk working at the time, in this moment of confusion, probably listed his name under this room number, imaging Oscar would be staying here."

"But he's not here," Liz said, glancing around.

"Here is the especially confusing aspect. I often stay in this very room but an out-of-towner actually had it when I first arrived. The clerk at the time of my arrival, who may or may not have been the clerk Oscar dealt with a few days later, more than likely, out of habit, wrote my name under this room number though I was actually sleeping in a room a few doors down. However, as you can see, the out-of-towner left, so the information at the desk that was wrong a few days ago is now right. It just shows all you have to do is wait."

Horace sighed and stepped forward. Liz placed a hand on his shoulder, pressing him gently back. "Thanks for clearing that up. But it still doesn't answer where he is."

A woman in a long blue dress with a beaded front entered the room carrying bags with greasy bottoms. "You must be Frank's friends." She placed the bags on the Formica table near the bookcases and took some china plates from a cabinet. "My name is Violet. It's so wonderful to meet you."

She placed the plates on the table and went up to them and stuck her hand out and Liz and Horace introduced themselves. The man she called Frank walked up behind them, cigarette in his fingers. "They arrived just in time. Only a few minutes ago, in fact." He placed the cigarette in his mouth, patted them on their backs. "Wash up. I hope you enjoy Chinese food."

Horace said, "We really just want to talk to Oscar."

"And I'm sure he wants to talk to you," Violet said as she opened the bags and placed the cartons beside the plates. "But have you two had dinner yet?"

Liz grinned and looked at Horace and said, "No, ma'am, we have not had a chance to have supper yet. We only got into town a while ago. There was a traffic jam at the tunnel."

"Then wash up and eat. How long of a drive is it from Memphis?"

"How did you know we're from Memphis?" asked Horace, stiffening.

"You're Oscar's friends, right?" She brought a handful of forks and spoons to the table. "I figured you must be from down there. That's where he has most of his friends."

Frank appeared again next to them, rolling up his sleeves and switching on the few lamps in the room. The shades all had a floral pattern with thick fringes hanging down, as if they'd been salvaged from a much earlier era. "You don't drive here, Frank?" Liz asked, washing her hands at the sink.

"Much too far for me." He lowered himself heavily into a chair at the table. "Also, when they finally condemn this place, which will be any day now, I want to be able to fly from here like a bird, not flee out of here like a rat. But if I was in your situation, I would probably drive too."

"And what exactly is our situation, Frank?" Horace asked.

"Young and free, with time on your hands."

"The first two would be right, but we that last one," Liz told him.

Horace was the last to take a seat. Liz kicked his foot

under the table and he kicked her back. Liz piled several spoonfuls of sesame chicken on to her mound of rice. "Eat up, Horace. You must be as hungry as I am."

"I like a woman with a good appetite," Frank told her, touching her arm. "Violet here eats like a bird. she thrives mainly off air, poetry, and cocaine."

"Yes, Frank. My holy trinity."

"Is Oscar expected here?" Horace asked. He had finally reached across the table to pick up the carton of rice.

"I suspect not. He and my daughter went to a jazz concert down on Bond Street. A place called Studio Dante. Violet and I were planning on joining them, and we might later on, but we haven't had a quiet night at home in a while."

Violet said, "This isn't really Frank's home. Don't let him fool you. He's a tourist in New York. He secretly prides himself on it."

"Violet, I feel like a tourist everywhere. That's why I'm always taking pictures." He tapped ash into a dirty wine glass on the windowsill behind his back.

"What kind of pictures do you take?" Liz asked, chewing on the chicken. She was surprised at how delicious she found the food.

"Scenes that most people would find boring," Violet said. "Cars sitting at the curb in the suburbs, a woman holding a cat in front of a gas station, the sky in Alabama, a diseased palm tree in New Orleans, a dog drinking water from a puddle in front of a Piggly Wiggly." She grinned at Frank and ran her hand along his hairy forearm and turned back to Liz. "Or maybe a kinder way of putting it would be he takes pictures of what most people would overlook."

Frank took a drag from his cigarette. "A friend of mine here in Manhattan says if you look at any one thing long enough, the meaning goes away. That's what interests me. Looking at something until the story behind it unravels and something else emerges. The world is filled with fascinating things if you scrape away the stupid stories we usually tell about those things."

Liz looked at Horace. Horace kept glancing at the half-open door to his right. She said, "You ain't hungry?"

"I'm hungry. I guess I just want to see Oscar more than you do."

Frank took a chicken leg out from one of the cartons. "Where do you know Oscar from?"

Liz said, "Tommy. I know him through Tommy. I was a big fan of Cosmic Dust. They really blew my mind back in the day."

Frank suddenly looked up at the doorway and said, "Why, there you are."

Horace bolted up from his seat and faced the doorway. Liz turned too and saw a woman with a gigantic fox fur around her shoulders coming into the room. She had hair the consistency of straw and a thin mustache over her mouth that she'd either drawn or tattooed. She went up to Horace and Liz, kissing both on the cheek. "Wonderful to see you again."

Horace sat down, wiping the spot where she had kissed with his napkin. "You don't know us."

"Valerie know everyone," said Frank. "She wakes up every other morning in a different country. She danced with Camus after the Liberation. She found van Gogh's ear for him when he cut it off."

"Are there any leftovers for me?" Valerie asked Violet.

Violet pointed to Horace. "This one isn't eating much. So there's plenty for you. Just pull up a seat."

Frank stood, gesturing to his chair, and Valerie took his place. Horace tapped Liz with his foot and through his gritted teeth murmured, "We need to go."

She nodded. "Let me just get two more bites. That was a long drive."

Frank sat back at the piano and looked out the window as if searching for inspiration in the buildings across the street. He started to play something classical. She didn't know what it was. As if reading her mind, he said, "Schubert. But I don't know this one very well. So if it sounds different from the

175

versions you've heard before just keep in mind I'll be making some of this up."

There was a gunshot about a block away. Both Liz and Horace stood instantly, Liz with her hand in her jacket pocket, fingers touching the handle of the switchblade. "You two are jumpy little fellows," Violet said, pouring more wine. "I thought this one was going to have a stroke when Valerie came in." She pointed to Horace.

"Don't worry," said Frank, his fingers still shifting across the piano keys. ""We're safe in here."

Violet drank from her glass, looking at Liz. "You must be hot in that jacket."

Liz removed her hand from her pocket. "I'm the kind of woman who likes to carry lots of things with her but I never took to purses. So this jacket with its pockets is my purse."

"Practical," said Valerie. She rubbed her fingers along the fox flung around her shoulders. "I wear this fur for similar and yet different reasons."

"We need to go," Horace said. "Thank you for the hospitality."

Liz asked Frank, "And what was that address on Bond Street again?"

"24 Bond Street. Look for a tall building between two short ones." He stopped playing and turned on the piano bench, crossing his legs. "Good luck finding them. If they're not there, they'll be someplace else."

She had parked the van in front of a building with shattered windows, a brick-strewn lot next to it. In the lot two teenagers with flashlights were kicking a ball back and forth. As they climbed into the van and slammed their doors, Liz said, "The girl we're not touching. Okay? Just Oscar."

"What are you talking about? There's no way Oscar hasn't told her everything. There's no way she doesn't know where Jimmy's house is."

"If we take care of Oscar, she'll be too scared to talk."

"Or she might be so pissed and hurt she will talk."

"That girl is that man's daughter."

"So we're not going to take care of business because her dad was nice to us? Think about what you're saying before you say it, Liz."

Liz looked at him, her hands on the steering wheel. He said, "What? What is it? I don't like it when you look at me like that."

She looked. She didn't move. She didn't twitch.

"Stop looking at me like that."

She reached over, tousled the yellow hair on his head. "Horace, you do not touch that girl. If you do, not only will I beat you to kingdom come, but I'll tell Vince all about how you sold those pictures of Edward Parker for some pocket change. Vince ain't going to be too happy about that. I know you think he's going to shrug it off, but I was the one to talk to him, and I know for a fact he ain't going to be shrugging this off. So you don't touch this girl, and we'll figure something out together regarding those pictures. You understand all this, right?"

"Yeah, Liz. I understand. Start the fucking van."

"You're like a brother to me, Horace, but you need to hear what I'm saying."

"I hear you. Now come on. Let's get out of here."

As she reached down and turned the key, she said, "22 Bond Street, here we come." She pulled away from the curb, glancing one more time at the two flashlights moving in the empty lot.

Chapter Twenty-Six

The stage consisted of a few pallets that had been arranged on the floor, with planks of plywood on top of them. A man with a white Afro and white neck beard played notes from his tenor saxophone, his nose dripping sweat and his eyes shut. There was a drummer behind him. Oscar watched from a leather club chair near the bar. His vision was blurry and his body felt like it was glowing with fever. Juanita sat on the arm of the chair, speaking with a man who said he was from Cuba. "It's a beautiful country with a terrible history," he was telling her. "But I guess most places are like that. I like to think of Cuba as a very special place. But it's only because I'm from there."

"Did you leave during the revolution?" Juanita asked.

"Before. I was in the States playing with a band. We were living in a hotel in California when all hell broke loose over there. We would get up early and buy a newspaper and take it to the beach and read about the awful things going on."

"Were you for Castro?"

"No. I wasn't for anybody. But that's only because I was here, in the States. Had I been there I would've had to chose sides."

Juanita asked, "And who do you think you would've chosen?"

"Whoever had the better taste in music."

Onstage the man with the neck beard kept sending out a scatter of notes into the air and then pausing, creating the sense of someone speaking rapidly and breathlessly and then stopping to gather in the next handful of ideas.

There were probably twenty listeners in the room. Most of them were black though there were a few in the audience who looked Cuban or Puerto Rican and there were three white guys on the fire escape behind him, smoking weed. Oscar reached up, tapped Juanita on the shoulder. "Let's go to that diner."

"You sure? You look even worse now than when we came in."

"I'm okay. We should at least drop by there, see if she's at the place tonight." He touched his forehead. It was blazing. He lied and said, "I think my fever's getting better anyway."

Juanita touched his forehead. "Oscar, you're only saying that because you want to go there. You're fever must be off the charts."

The man she'd been speaking with looked down at him. "You need something? I have some things on me that might make you feel better?"

"What do you have?" Oscar asked.

Juanita shook her head. "He's not taking anything. He just needs some rest."

"I have aspirin. I have Tylenol. The air in this city gives me headaches. It's like a pot of boiling water with a lid on top of it, keeping the steam in."

"When you said things that might make him feel better, I thought you were talking about something else" Juanita said.

"So you imagined I was a drug dealer?"

"No. Just someone very generous with what he might have on hand."

"I'll take some aspirin," Oscar said.

The man went through the pockets of his tweed jacket and took out a bottle. "Take the whole thing. There's only a couple left." He handed the bottle to Oscar and Oscar shook two capsules out into his palm and reached down, picking up the glass bottle of Tab at his feet. He swallowed them. He nodded thanks to the man, placing the pill bottle in the pocket of his jeans.

On the sidewalk, Oscar asked, "Let's walk. It's only a few blocks away."

"In your condition? You look like you can barely stand."

"The aspirins should kick in soon."

"Like they're going to do very much."

As they rode in the cab, Oscar said, "You should've stayed there. That guy was really into you."

"The music was giving me a headache. I know I'm supposed to like music like that but I don't."

Oscar said, "I was enjoying it."

"You were not. You're only being contrarian."

"I was enjoying it. Jazz like that, it's trying to get you to think with a different part of your brain."

"My brain thinks fine as it is."

"What they're doing and what they're doing at CBGB isn't that different. They're responding to the same vibrations out there in the air."

"And have you ever seen me at that club either?"

"I've invited you more than once."

"You could catch syphilis just touching the walls in that place."

They passed a building with gray smoke billowing from the top of it. A group of teenagers stood across the street, some of them holding baseball bats over their shoulders and one of them clutching a golf club. They watched the smoke, pointed at it. A burst of flame blew out through one of the windows on the top floor. The taxi driver drove by the scene, shaking his head. He turned right at Houston Street and soon they were passing two fire trucks speeding along in the opposite direction. "I hate this city," he told them in an Eastern European accent. "No one works anymore. All they do is start fires and throw stones at the police. You can't even take your grandchildren to a park anymore. It's nothing but needles and filth.."

"It'll get better," Juanita said. "These things come and go."

"I almost don't want it to get better. The city doesn't

deserve to get better."

They got out at the corner of Essex and Houston. A few buildings down they found the delicatessen Samuel had told them about and they went inside. Oscar searched the faces of the few patrons: none of them were Diana. There were a few old men and a table of Latino women in their fifties in summer dresses and makeup and a black man in a back booth in a pink polo shirt, reading a paperback. Oscar and Juanita took the booth across from him. Oscar sneezed again, removing the handkerchief from his back pocket. He wanted a cigarette but his throat was sore and he suspected smoking would make it worse. "I'm not that hungry," he said.

"I would've been surprised if you were."

The door of the bathroom opened and Oscar glanced up. He saw her. Except it wasn't her. Diana was not in her dress, not in her makeup. She had her hair tied back in a bun and had not shaved in a few days. Diana looked at him and he looked away. Diana slid into the booth with the guy in the polo shirt. Oscar looked at Juanita, who was looking across at the booth too. Diana turned, flashed them a cool smile, and said, "Do I know you two? You can't seem to take your eyes off of me." She spoke with a husky feminine voice with an exaggerated southern lilt.

"Are you Diana?" Juanita asked before Oscar could.

"That would be one of my names. You see my show at some point?"

"No," Oscar said, placing his tattered menu back on the table. "We never caught the show. I think you might've known a friend of ours, though, down in Memphis. You ever meet a guy named Tommy? A white guy with a lot of dark hair who usually wore a yin yang symbol on his neck?"

The expression on her face turned from distant warmth to cold stone. "What do you two want? I have nothing to say about Memphis. I left there for good and I ain't ever going back to that shithole."

"I'm not trying to stir anything up," Oscar said. "I just

wanted to let you know, if you didn't know already, that Tommy's dead. He died of an overdose in Arizona a few weeks back."

"I didn't know. That's really too bad. He seemed like a good guy who got mixed up in shit he never should've been mixed up in."

The man across from Diana tapped her on the elbow. "If these guys are bothering you I can escort them to the door."

Diana nodded no. "It's all right."

Oscar said, "Diana, he had a message he wanted me to give you. He said he's sorry. I don't know what he was sorry about. He didn't tell me. He just told me to tell you he's sorry." He could feel Juanita staring at him.

Diana looked at Oscar. Eventually she said, "He had nothing to apologize for. He wasn't the one to set things up. From what I understood he didn't have much of a choice. He owed certain people."

"Liz?"

"Yeah. You know her too?"

"I do though I wish I didn't."

"How about Randy? You know Randy?"

"We've met him," said Juanita.

"I used to go around with Randy. I was the one to tell him about the guy whose name I never mention anymore. I complained about this person. He treated me so good on some nights but others he hated me. I was this symbol of everything he hated about himself. He loved me but he hated the fact he loved me. So one night he'd run warm and the other he'd run cold. He never laid a hand on me. I don't mean to imply that. He never struck me. But what he'd say to me some nights used to sting. It used to hurt so much."

"You're talking about Edward Parker?" Oscar asked.

Diana's hands shot up to her ears, covering them. Then she placed one finger over her mouth and hushed him. "Do not ever say that name in my presence again. I take no pleasure in the fact he killed himself. I don't. I wish he never did that to himself. But he wrecked me. He pretended to love me and maybe he did but he wrecked me just the same. He hated himself and due to that hate he wrecked me."

"You don't have to go into this shit," said the man in the booth with her.

"I'm almost done." She undid the bun at the back of her scalp, shaking her hair out and combing it with her long nails until it was parted in the middle. "That's better. More relaxing." To Oscar and Juanita, she said, "I'm leaving here soon. I'm moving to Berlin. If I didn't already have one foot outside this goddamn country I don't think I'd be sitting here, talking to you in this manner. But the past has a little less weight when you're about to turn your back on it."

"Why are you going to Berlin?" asked Juanita.

"It seems like the place to be. It's right at the seam of the world, you know? It's hard to explain in a way that doesn't make me sound like a nutcase, but for the past few years I can't get that place out of my mind. And I hardly even know a thing about it."

"You speak German?" asked Oscar.

"I've picked some up from watching foreign films. And the occasional language book here and there." Diana lifted her legs and placed them on the seat, crossing them at the calves. "I just have one more thing to say about Memphis. I've heard some of those pictures are circulating though I've never seen any myself. I've also heard in those pictures you can't see my face though you can see other parts of my anatomy. If you see Liz again, tell her that was not part of the deal. We all knew he whose name I will not speak would pay. There was never a chance he wouldn't. I only agreed to the whole thing under the condition that those pictures never be released. So tell Liz to take care of it. I'm a private person. I realize it might not seem like it but I am. I do not like images of parts of my body floating out there, even if no face is attached."

"I'm sure I'll see Liz soon and I'll bring it up with her."

"Thank you. Even if I'm across the ocean, I still care about these things."

A waitress stepped out from the kitchen, straightening her uniform shirt. As she came down the aisle toward Oscar and Juanita, Oscar heard the bell over the door jingle. At first the waitress blocked his view of who had walked in. But as she neared their booth he could again see up the aisle to the front of the room. "Oh, Jesus," he said. Liz and a man he did not know stood at the entrance. The man was dressed in a Kiss T-shirt and wore sunglasses. Juanita turned to see what Oscar was staring at. Then Diana turned and the man Diana was with looked up. All four were looking at Liz and the man. Liz said, "Good morning everyone."

The dozen or so other people in the delicatessen stopped speaking and stopped eating and turned their heads to look at her. "Long time no see, Diana," she said loud enough for her voice to carry through that long, narrow space.

Diana glared over at Oscar. "Was this all some kind of trick?"

"Not at all," he said. "I don't know how they knew I was here."

Liz heard them. "We followed you from that place over on Bond Street. We have a big white van and we were only a few cars behind you but I guess you're not real good checking to see if you're being followed."

The waitress hollered over to Liz, "You want to sit with these people? Might make talking to them easier."

Liz looked at the man she was with and he nodded to her and she nodded to him. They walked down the aisle, Liz first. Diana stood, picking up the plaid satchel that'd been under the table. She rose just as Liz and the man walked up. "You join us, Diana," Liz told her. "It'll be like some big reunion."

"These people were telling me about Tommy," Diana said, placing the satchel under her arm. "They told me he died from an overdose out west somewhere. I was sorry to hear that. He wasn't like you two. I actually liked him."

"It was in a seedy little hotel room in Tucson. That's where he died," the man in the sunglasses said.

"Yeah," said Diana. "Because you assholes chased him there."

"You need to be very careful what you say tonight," the man in the sunglasses told her. "Me and Liz are not in the mood."

Liz smiled. She said, "Diana, sit with us for a while. It'll give us a chance to hash things out so we won't ever have to do it again."

Diana continued standing. The man in the polo shirt rose from the booth too. He and Liz and Diana and the men with the sunglasses all stared hard at each other in the center of the aisle. The waitress said, "If you all aren't going sit down, then I can't take your order." As she moved hurriedly toward the kitchen doorway, she said, "Let me know when you're ready." Oscar mouthed to Juanita, "Go," and he pointed to the door several feet behind them. It was propped open with a wedge of wood. Juanita grabbed a fork and knife from the table, dropping them into her evening bag. She slipped out the door as Diana was saying, "You can't tell me what to do, Liz. You never really could." She turned to the man in sunglasses and said, "Step aside, young man."

"Fuck you, faggot," said the man in sunglasses.

The man in the polo shirt started for the man in the sunglasses but Liz held up her hand and said, "No, let's not do this. My friend here is not particularly couth. He doesn't mean any harm."

Oscar said, "Liz, sit down. You and your little buddy there with the sensitive eyes, both of you sit down. You came here for me, not them."

Liz gave Diana a nasty, menacing look. She sat in the booth and scooted to the wall and the man in sunglasses turned his face toward the man in the polo shirt and grimaced and followed Liz into the booth. Both of them were across from Oscar. Diana said, "You guys did not keep your promise about the pictures. I want them off the street, you hear?"

"I thought you were going to Kiev or someplace," said the

man with the sunglasses. "So why would you care?"

"It's Berlin. But I still don't want them out there."

Liz said, "I'll do what I can."

Diana glanced over at Oscar. "You going to be all right?"

"I'll be fine."

"Thank you for the message. I didn't know Tommy very well but I liked the little bit of him I did know."

Liz looked over at her. "You haven't been telling your friends about your adventures in Memphis, have you now?"

Diana glanced at the man in the polo shirt next to her. To Liz, she said, "Go to hell, Liz. And you too, Horace. I'm done with both of you. I wish I never saw your faces and I wish I never heard your names." She and the man walked down the aisle and through the front door. The delicatessen was empty now: only the three of them in the booth.

Twenty-Seven

"We've never had the pleasure of meeting," said the man with the sunglasses. "My name is Horace, as you could probably tell from that exchange." He picked up his menu, not offering his hand.

"I'm Oscar. But you already know that."

"We've come a long way to see you, Oscar," said Liz.

"And I've come a long way to get away from you. We've both traveled the same distance, I guess."

"What happened to your lady friend?" asked Horace.

"She remembered she had to be elsewhere."

"Busy people in this city." Horace scratched his cheek.

"Sure are," Oscar replied.

Liz tapped her finger against the tabletop as if to get his attention. "I have to apologize for what happened at Jimmy's place a few days ago, Oscar. That was uncalled for on Walter's part. Walter is a guy who has been in our hair off and on for many a year. On that particular day, he decided to take his anger with us one step further."

"It gave me a chance to get out of that place, so I don't hold anything against him. Far as I'm concerned he was doing me a favor."

Liz interlaced her fingers and placed them on the table and leaned forward. Her leather jacket creaked. The metal studs around its collar seemed to shine from the fluorescent lights but he knew it might simply be his fever creating that effect. She asked, "I bet you wish it was him instead of me who left

---

187

that place still walking, don't you? You can be honest. I think for tonight we should be as honest with one another as possible, don't you think?"

Oscar sneezed. He grabbed a handful of napkins from the napkin dispenser. As he wiped his nose, he told her, "I don't wish anybody dead. I'm a true child of the sixties that way."

"We're a long way from the sixties," Horace said.

"And soon we'll be a long way from the seventies. So what?" He tucked the wet napkins into his pocket and asked, "Richard told a friend of mine he delivered a special package to Tommy and I'd really like to know, before we go on to anything else, what that special package might've been."

Liz said, "I don't have to answer that." Her cheek quivered as she said it.

"I thought we were being honest tonight."

Liz cracked her knuckles, looking at him.

Oscar continued, "Richard thought he was delivering just another bag of heroin. That's what he meant by 'special package.' But I've been thinking of that phrase over and over again and I've come to believe it means something more than he intended. Richard is no killer and even if he were you'd never trust him with an assignment like this, would you, Liz?"

She licked her lips and smiled. "Let's go on to more relevant topics."

"You killed him. You two knew how bad he felt about the Edward Parker deal, especially after he killed himself, and you two lived in terror that he might take the whole thing to the police. Chances are, if I know Tommy, he even made some threats off and on, saying he would take it to the cops. Because when Tommy got emotional he just blurted shit out. He would say whatever was in his head, consequences be damned."

Both Liz and Horace glared at him.

"And what makes it worse is that he doesn't want money, he doesn't request an extra few hundred for him to keep his mouth shut. No. It's not about the money. It's guilt. All that religious stuff comes back to bite him on the ass. Yin and Yang comes back to bite him on the ass. God comes back to bite him on the ass. St. Teresa comes back to bite him on the ass. He can't live with what he did and you know it and he knows you know it. So you two start to threaten him. Maybe you rough him up one night, telling him if he goes to the police he'll pay the price. Maybe. I don't know. Or maybe you thought nothing would send him to the police quicker than roughing him up. But somehow, you hound him. You hound him out of Memphis and that's why he vanishes one night and heads out west. That's how he winds up in that seedy Tucson apartment."

Liz licked her lips again. "He's good, Horace. Ain't he good? He has thought this whole thing out, top to bottom."

Horace stared at him through his sunglasses.

Oscar took more napkins from the dispenser, wiped his nose again. His body felt like a single shivering muscle. He said, "You didn't put the needle in his arm, no, but you had a little extra something in that baggie."

"He killed himself," Horace said. "He did it just as surely as someone puts a gun to their temple and squeezes the trigger."

"What do you mean?" Oscar asked.

"You dumb shit," Liz said. "Tommy was like ole man river. He was tired of living but afraid of dying. But by the end he was less afraid of dying than he was tired of living. Everything you said up to now is true. Good for you. You had a few of the puzzle pieces and you worked it out. But when he injected himself with that smack he knew exactly what he was doing."

"You told him?"

Liz placed her hands palms down on the table. "I spoke with him, told him Richard was coming. Over the phone I could hear how bad off he was. I reckon it was a combination of all the drugs and the guilt and him wanting to go to the cops to turn himself in and him being afraid of it and him being afraid of us too. His voice was this tiny whisper, this rasp. So I told him, 'Tommy, I'm sending this special package your way. I got some real good shit, just for you.' I told it was going to be like nothing he'd experienced before. It was going to take all his troubles away and smooth his worried brow and all that shit. I said, 'Tommy, it's just for you. Don't give Richard any. He's going to beg for a taste but don't you let him.' I said, 'In fact, Tommy, just wait until he's gone, because knowing Richard he might sneak behind your back and steal some of this real good shit from you.' That's what I told him. And he kept saying, 'Yeah, sure, I understand.' And he did too. He understood what I was telling him."

"You can tell it to yourself however you want," Oscar said, blowing his nose. "But you hounded him. You stepped on him. You made it so he didn't have any choice but to put that stuff in his veins. I've hung around some slime balls in my life but I've never hung around the likes of you two."

"You better be careful, what you say," said Horace.

"Screw you," Oscar told him.

"Really? You're really going to sit there and dare to say that shit to my face, you fucking asshole." Horace removed is sunglasses, hanging them on the neck of his T-shirt.

Before Oscar could reply, Liz said, "Tommy knew. He wanted to go. And you need to let him go too."

"You seem to think him knowing lets you off the hook. It doesn't. It's like giving some guy two options. He can either shoot himself in the head or he can have you shoot him in the head. That's not much of a choice. And you'd be hard pressed to find someone out there who'd call it one."

Her cheek twitched again. She cleared her throat and jutted her chin out. "Oscar, I'm done talking with you in here. You need to come with us. We have the van outside."

"Now why in the hell would I go with you to the van?"

Horace shifted in his seat and swung an arm behind his back and when his arm reappeared he was pointing a shiny black revolver at Oscar's head. "Hold on, now," said Oscar, throwing hands up in surrender. "You don't need that."

"You coming with us?" asked Liz.

"I'd rather not. I like it in here. Lots of windows."

Horace stood from the booth and brought the tip of the gun closer to Oscar's head. "Get up. The van will be fine. You've been in it before."

"I have," Oscar said. "That's why I don't really want to go in it again." He felt if he moved from the booth it would be over. He had to talk. He had to keep talking. He had to stay here, where there were windows. Now that Horace had his gun out someone would notice him through the glass and phone the police. Maybe Juanita was outside, watching, waiting to see if Liz and Horace would go harmlessly into the night. Maybe she had been waiting for some final indication about whether or not to get help.

"I'm going to count to three," Horace said. "I don't have any qualms about blowing you away right here and now."

"Liz, get him to stop," Oscar said.

"I can't, Oscar. It's too late."

"One," he said.

"Stop him," Oscar said.

"You stop him by coming with us," Liz said. "Right now."

"Okay," Oscar said. "I'll go with you."

Horace grinned over his gun and began to lower it when the top of his head exploded into hundred of hairy bits across Oscar and the booth and Liz. Oscar felt blood in matter in his mouth, his eyes. The body of Horace stood for several seconds with everything above the nose missing. Then it fell where it stood, collapsing like a puppet whose strings have been snipped by a single cut of the scissors. A man in white pants and a white T-shirt and white apron stood in the kitchen doorway, holding a rifle. He was breathing so hard he looked like he'd only just then stopped running for miles.

Oscar spat on the floor, wiping his mouth with his blood-covered forearm. He could hear bits of Horace drip from the wall and ceiling. He. He heard Liz say, "You fucking asshole." He heard gunshots. When he looked up he saw Liz falling, her foot having slipped on the blood. The man from the kitchen vanished from the room as if he'd never been in it. The gunshots Liz fired had landed clumsily on the wall over the kitchen doorway.

Twenty-Eight

Oscar ran to the back door, where Juanita had left earlier. He heard steps following him. He ran down the block, past two streetlights. One gave no light at all and the other flickered frantically. As he turned right on Stanton he glanced back and saw her running in his direction, a long gun in her hand. He kept on, moving east, flying by three buildings with boarded windows. He heard a shot. He found himself flat against the sidewalk. He felt no pain. He stood again without looking behind his back and took off down an empty lot over stones and boards and past a car door and started climbing the chainlink fence at the back of the lot. In the darkness he could barely see the fence, he mostly felt it as he lifted his leg over the sharp edges at the top. There was another shot. The bullet hit a brick wall not far from his leg. His inner thigh scraped hard against the sharp points at the top of the fence as he fell to the other side, landing on his back. He gritted his teeth. His back and thigh were in agony. To his left he heard her make her way, her feet sounding against a plank of wood not far from the fence.

He made his legs stand. Blood dribbled down his thigh as he ran around the corner of another boarded up building. As he crouched in the doorway he touched his inner thigh. It was too dark to see his hand but he could feel the wet against his palm. A voice said, "Buddy, what're you doing there?" It came from behind him, inside the room beyond the doorway. A flashlight snapped on and its beam struck his eyes and he blinked in the brightness of it. The man holding the flashlight asked, "You ain't here to rob me, are you? Because I tell you what, I ain't got nothing you want to rob." He laughed hoarsely. The laugh turned into a cough. He added, "Is it Saturday night? Always seems like we get a lot more people running around here, Saturday nights."

Oscar limped into the room. He said, "Could you point me to the stairs?"

The beam shifted, lighting the mouth of a dark corridor. "Down there to your left. I'd be careful if I was you, though. Some real loony ones up there. Anybody give you any trouble you tell them Leroy sent you."

Oscar could hear the outside fence clanging. Then he heard it stop clanging. She'd made the jump. He limped as fast as the wound in his thigh allowed him, moving to where the man was shining the beam. The corridor smelled of shit and dust. It was hot too. He could feel the heat of it through his chills. He stumbled over a pair of legs and felt hands grab his knee but he kept on, pulling away from the person on the floor. The figure sobbed. She yelled out after him, "You can't just treat people like that! You hear me! You got to say excuse me! I'm a human being too, you jerk!"

He went through a doorway, into what appeared to be a vestibule. There was a broken window in the wall and through it shined the glow of a streetlight. From its glow he could make out the first steps of the staircase.

Just as he was about to climb it he heard gunshots outside. He heard two shots fired and silence and another shot fired. He heard a scream. It was a woman screaming but he couldn't tell if it was Liz or not. Then there was another shot, followed by more silence. He waited, his foot on the first step. When he heard steps along the back of the building he forced himself to start climbing. The wound in his thigh bit deep into his flesh and his teeth chattered with fever. He limped up one flight of stairs and then another. There was ringing in his ears and his stomach muscles clenched. To his left was a lit room. He moved toward it.

In the room several votive candles had been lit and placed in the corners and along the windowsill. There was a mattress with a young man and woman curled up together on it, both of them facing the wall. Oscar sat in the far corner of the room. He had to rest: the pain and the fever bore down upon him. The ringing in his ears grew louder and soon it seemed to be flooding through his head and as it ebbed away he opened his eyes and looked at Tommy. Tommy crouched near him, his yin yang medallion hanging from his chest. Oscar tried to smile. "She's going to kill me just like she killed you."

Tommy looked at him with a bemused expression. "You should've come out to visit me in Arizona. It was incredible. I'd drop acid and me and some of the friends I made there would drive out to the desert in the middle of the night and watch the sun rise."

"Sounds fun. Wish I did go."

"I met Maria out there. I think I did, at least. My memories of her are always so hazy. But to tell you the truth, my memories of a lot of shit are hazy these days. You know, Oscar, I'm in this weird place now, man. What was before is now after, and I can't ever seem to find the middle at all."

"Same here, Tommy."

Tommy stood, flicking his hair from his face with his long pale hand. "We once fucked in the desert, me and Maria. Right out in the open air. It was night and it was windy and we were out under the stars. She brought this towel with her. Her hair kept on blowing, getting in my mouth. This was when I was starting to realize how moving to Tucson wasn't going to fix anything. This was when I started to realize I couldn't bear being around myself anymore and no matter how far I went I never was going to shake myself."

"Tommy, there's probably no way you could help me out here, is there?"

Tommy shook his head. He flashed Oscar the peace sign, as he sometimes did when he was leaving at the end of a party, or going home after a night at the bar. "Maria says to tell you hi. I'm glad you had a chance to meet her. Though between you and me, she's always scared me a little."

"Why is that?"

"Because she never told me her last name no matter how me times I asked her. And for all I know, Maria might've been a name she just made up."

"Did you know her when you were kids?"

"Sometimes it seems like I did, sometimes I'm not so sure. Like I said, these days the middle is missing. I know one thing, though."

"Yeah, Tommy?"

"You need to see the desert before you die, man. You never have seen it, have you?"

"Never have. I flew into Los Angeles a few times and saw it from up high. But never up close."

"See it up close. It'll be worth the trip."

Tommy strode through the doorway and his shape blended into the darkness of the stairwell. He made no sound. He was no longer there.

Oscar took three big breaths and hoisted himself up, pressing his back to the wall. As he limped he could feel the blood squish around in his sneaker. He moved in the direction Tommy had gone and listened. He heard Liz yell and he heard a man yell though both yells were unclear. Then he heard the man yell, "Give that back!" And he heard Liz yell, "I'll fucking shoot your hand off if you don't let go."

There was no more yelling.

Oscar continued up the next flight of stairs, and then another. There was a tiny dead bird on the next step. Oscar kicked it off with his tennis shoe, watching it fall through the stairwell shaft like a piece of plaster. It landed right in front of the flashlight beam. Liz turned the beam up in the direction of where the body had come from. Oscar moved away from the banister before the beam reached him. Instead, it continued up until reaching the top of the stairwell. He followed the beam with his eyes and realized there were only three more floors to go. Liz called up, "I hear you. There's no place to escape up there. Why don't you come down and we can talk." He could hear her boots clacking up the steps below him. He could hear her huffing. "I was shooting you out of shock. I've calmed down now, Oscar. Horace was a friend. When I saw him get shot I think I went a little berserk."

He walked up the next few steps. The leg with the thigh wound was becoming more difficult to move and his fever was tearing through his body with chills and aches and his throat was so sore he could barely swallow. He called down, "If you're going kill me you're going to have to work for it. As far as your friend, fuck him. I just wish that'd been you too."

A shot rang up into the stairwell, the bullet chipping the banister one floor below him before crashing through one of the windows. "He was my friend, asshole!" she yelled. "Don't talk about him like that."

Doors started to slam shut through up and down the building. A woman's voice called out from some dark spot above him, "If I had a goddamn phone I'd call the goddamn cops!"

"You hear that, Liz!" he yelled, keeping his back against the wall as he struggled with every step. "You're waking up the entire building."

"When I first met Tommy, you'd know what we'd do?" she said, the beam of her flashlight again wandering up the stairwell in search of his face. "We'd listen to Low. What an album that is. It's true I think Big Black Chevelle is the better record. But Low stays with you more. Low is Tommy saying goodbye." She paused, huffing. Oscar thought he felt a breeze coming from above but it was too dark to see anything. All around him was darkness. The only light that broke that darkness was the flashlight beam that occasionally played over the banister near him. Liz added, "Tommy would tell me how you fucked it up. He said Low could have been a great record if you hadn't decided you wanted to wreck each song with a bunch of noise and shit."

"Maybe he was right. But too late to tell now, right?"

Another voice shouted from the dark. "Get out of here! This is unacceptable! You're waking everybody up!"

Oscar glanced quickly down at the beam and realized Liz was gaining ground. She was going faster than him. He yelled, "Liz, if you liked Tommy so much, why did you get him involved in the whole thing?"

"I'd rather talk about you, Oscar. I'd rather talk about how pissed off Tommy would get some nights when him and me and Randy were hanging out. I'd rather talk about how he'd snort some coke and ramble on for hours about how you and him could've shaken up the scene but you just turned your back on him!" She coughed, the flashlight dropping from her grip. It rolled down the steps and rolled off into the stairwell shaft, crashing on the ground floor. Oscar held his hand up in front of him. There was a breeze another flight up. He had no doubts now.

"He'd be alive if he never met you," Oscar said. He balled his fists and took another few steps, forcing himself past the pain in his thigh. Sweat had bathed his body and soaked his clothes.

Liz continued talking, projecting her voice up the stairwell shaft. "Did you know David Bowie did an album called Low last year? You realize that? Must be something about that title. It gets around."

"Probably speaks to how a lot of us are feeling."

She was only a flight and a half below him. He took another three steps, straining, and could see a sliver of light only a few more steps ahead. As he made those final steps he heard the sirens. At first he heard one, and then two, and then he heard three or four. As he pushed open the door and stepped on to the roof he saw blue police lights on the walls of the buildings across the street. He looked around the rooftop for an object he could hold tight in his grip. There were broken plates and a tattered lampshade and a dead rat that had dried in the June sun and part of a TV antenna. It was the antenna he picked up. Steps were coming closer to

198

the door. He limped to the side of it and listened so hard his head ached and he heard the steps at the threshold and the hand holding the gun appeared through the doorway and with his entire weight behind it he swung the antenna across the wrist and the hand released the gun.

He plunged into her back, whipping the antenna along the back of her head. She kicked him off, lurching forward and pounding him with her fist. He fell face first into the gravel and debris. A voice echoed up through the stairwell and past the open rooftop door: it was Juanita's voice, and she was yelling, "Oscar! Oscar, are you all right! I called the police! Oscar, they're coming up!"

He turned and saw Liz holding the gun at his head. In the light of the red sky above them he could see a trickle of blood had dripped down from her jacket and across her jeans. She saw him staring at it. She smiled. "Grazed by a bullet twice in three days. You think God is trying to get my attention?" She touched the wound at her side. She lifted up her bloodied fingertips for him to see. "It was the kitchen cook again, trying to be some fucking hero of the day. You believe that shit? He came around the corner when I was climbing that fence. He almost got me. If I was just a little bit slower he would've."

"Put the gun down, Liz. There's no reason to keep on doing this. You're not like Horace." He could hear many, many steps rushing up the stairwell. He knew she could hear it too. But she kept the gun on him, the red sky glowing just beyond her as if it were her element.

"Tommy could be so sweet," said Liz. "The fucked up thing about me is that I didn't know how to handle it. I wanted to get near him, and I did. I got near him the way I always get near people. By fucking up their lives. By burning down their houses. By hitting them in the back of their fucking heads."

"Liz, please. Don't squeeze that trigger."

"Oscar, I'm not going to kill you. Not now, at least. It's too late. Plus, I like some of the songs you once wrote.

You're not a completely worthless piece of shit." She turned to the two police officers rushing at her. She pointed the pistol at them and they said drop the fucking gun and she smiled and raised the barrel slightly and shot into the sky over their heads. But the police had already fired, her body was already crashing through space and falling from the rooftop. Oscar covered his ears so as not to hear her land in the street below. An officer jogged up to him, tucking his gun away. "You all right, mister?" he asked.

Oscar nodded. Then he covered his face and tried to catch his breath. "Dude here is bleeding bad in his leg," the cop said to another cop behind him. "Let's get a paramedic up here quick, guys."

A hand touched his arm and he could tell it wasn't the cop's. As he lowered his hands he saw Juanita crouching beside him. "The fork and knife didn't come in very handy."

"Yeah, once the guns come out, they don't help much."

"You know the crazy thing? I didn't have any change. I had to run way down a side street to a Laundromat to get change to call the cops."

"You should start carrying some quarters, at least."

He turned from her and vomited. The ringing returned to his ears but through the ringing he heard her say everything would be all right now.

Twenty-Nine

In early August the days reached a hundred and heat rippled the air over the sidewalks and streets and when you walked through a neighborhood it was quiet with the exception of the air-conditioners humming in the windows. Frank held a birthday party for Juanita on the sixth of the month. He bought ribs and ground beef and hired a man who worked at the Leahy's BBQ on Summer Avenue to cook. The guest started to arrive at dusk. Oscar got there around nine. When Frank shook his hand, he said, "Glad you could make it. You haven't been around much lately."

"You know me. Sometimes I'm busy as hell. And sometimes all I do is sit in my room and drink."

"You're a mysterious one, Oscar."

"More lazy than mysterious, I think."

"I was wondering if I could ask a favor. I'm flying back up to New York again next week. You think you could give me a lift to the airport?"

"Yeah. I can do that. Just tell me when."

"Of course, you're welcome to come up too."

Oscar took a Miller Lite from the metal tub packed with ice. As he pulled back the tab, he said, "Maybe not this time. Sometime, though." He and Juanita had told Frank the entire bloody affair had been a case of mistaken identity: Liz and Horace thought Oscar was a guy who'd crossed them in a drug deal. They told the police the same. And since there were several other grisly homicides in Manhattan that night, they were willing to believe them.

Oscar circulated through the party. Brian was by the BBQ smoker. He asked Oscar when he wanted to return to the studio to finish up the record. "We're so close, man. I think it'll only take another three or four sessions."

"I just haven't been in the spirit of it," Oscar explained. The one time he'd returned to the studio after that night in the building he'd started to sweat when yelling his vocals into the microphone. His hands trembled. Yelling brought back that climb up the staircase, with the flashlight beam dancing over the banisters and walls in search of his face. He swallowed some beer and added, "Maybe once the weather cools down. Maybe when it's not summer anymore I'll be able to get my head back together."

Brian patted him on the back. He knew about the New York shootout but not about Tommy or Edward Parker. The only other person who knew was Juanita. And Diana. And Maria, whoever she was and wherever she might be.

In the arbor at the back fence where banks of blue phlox grew his aunt Sophie sat in a wicker chair listening to a young woman play guitar and sing folk ballads. He hadn't seen her in months. She lived in a house on Central Avenue but spent much of her time in Oxford, Mississippi, with her beau, a history professor at the University. There were a few friends in other wicker chairs around her. When she saw Oscar, though, she called him over. "Oscar, don't you know you should be drinking cocktails at an event like this?"

"I like to drink with the masses."

"Bullshit. If everyone were drinking Miller Lites you'd be the first to order a Negroni. I wanted to ask you: what's this I hear about you almost getting my daughter killed in New York?"

He took a large sip of beer. He still didn't like talking about it, thinking back on it. "It was a hell of a thing," he told her. "Juanita was never really in danger though, far as I know. I'm the son of a bitch they wanted."

"And all because you looked like this other guy?" She eyed

him skeptically.

"So they said. The two thugs chasing me, I mean."

"Couldn't you've simply showed them your driver's license? It seems like that would've cleared the matter up."

"It wasn't the kind of situation where you could sit down and discuss things rationally." He looked down at his beer can, then back at her. "Maybe we should talk about something else."

She squeezed his elbow. "Of course, Oscar. I'm just glad you made it through that night alive."

"I'm fairly happy about that too."

An hour later he noticed Frank going around with the Sony Portapak camera he'd bought recently. He wandered barefoot through the yard, filming the scene. When Frank approached him with the Portapak, Frank said, "You have anything to add, young man?"

Oscar nodded no. "Everything has already been said."

Later in the night he sat with the folk singer on her blanket and borrowed her guitar and strummed a few Beatles' melodies. He handed the guitar back and she sang some Joni Mitchell songs from Blue. They went into the house and made out on the sofa in the den and she said she had to get back outside because she was getting paid to perform at the party and Oscar asked how she knew Frank and she said her and Frank had had some really good times over the years and she smiled mischievously at him and buttoned her gauzy blouse and left.

In the kitchen Oscar opened the refrigerator door, grabbed the tin holding a slice of cherry cobbler, and ate it with his hands over the sink. Juanita walked in with her date for the night, a broad-shouldered guy in law school at Memphis State. Oscar could never remember his name. "There you are," she said. "It seems like we keep missing each other tonight. Every time I'm talking to one group of people you're over there talking to another."

He wiped his hands and mouth with a paper towel. "Well, here I am." He added, chewing, "Happy birthday."

"I really didn't want Dad to do all this."

Oscar didn't say what he was thinking, which was that Frank had been shaken by what happened in New York and at the idea he'd accidentally directed two criminals to the whereabouts of his daughter and nephew. Oscar suspected this party was Frank's way of trying to put the dangers of that night behind them.

Juanita turned to her date and asked if they could be alone for a minute. After he left, she asked Oscar, "Brian told me you're still a no-show at the studio. You planning on having the record exist in a perpetually unfinished state? Like some unfinished symphony?"

"Nothing that grand. I just haven't been in the mood. I'm hoping that'll change when the weather turns."

"I'm flying up with Dad to New York. Did you know that?"

"I did not. I guess I'll be driving both of you to the airport then."

"I don't like being afraid. And I know that until I see those places again in the full light of day I will be."

"Sounds like a good reason to go."

"You could come too."

"I don't have a ticket."

"Dad could help you out."

He shook his head. "I tell you I got my old job back? Flipping pancakes over at KC's Café? I'm right back where I started from."

"Not really, though, right?"

He shrugged in response. Outside, some of the guests were singing "Fly Me to the Moon." Oscar took a small package wrapped in Christmas paper from his pocket. He handed it to Juanita. "Happy Birthday."

She tore the paper away and opened the top of the rectangular box. She slid a knife and fork into her palm. She stared at them. She looked up. "Little good these did us."

"I don't know. You still saved my life."

"I'm sure other people were calling around the same time I

did."

"Maybe so. Maybe not. But you definitely did."

"You told me yourself she had her chance but didn't take it."

"The police added a certain amount of panic to her night, I'm sure. She knew she'd never get back to her van soon as she heard them on those steps."

Juanita took the fork and knife and dropped them in her purse. "I'll keep them. I don't think that delicatessen would mind."

"You know, we never tried the food there."

"I'll let you know how it is."

She took a few steps toward the door. "Do you think Diana made it to Berlin? You think she actually went?"

"Yeah, I do. I think seeing Liz and Horace probably made her want to go all the more."

Juanita glanced out the window at all the guests who'd gathered for her party. "They're never going to know the real story about Tommy."

"Makes you wonder if it was worth it, doesn't it?"

"Tommy wanted us to know, don't you think?"

"I guess he did. Though I suspect he had no idea how much trouble it'd cause. Or maybe he was so baked on drugs, he just didn't realize. I can't imagine he would've wanted us to go through all that."

"That's right. He was probably just flailing in Tucson. He probably sent those messages to us without really knowing why."

She walked through the French doors and down the terrace. Oscar threw his empty beer can into the trash and wandered further back into the house. He turned off the lamp in the den and tossed himself on to the sofa and placed his hands over his eyes. There were times these past weeks when he needed suddenly to be alone. There were times when he needed to sit in a dark room and be by himself. From outside he could hear everyone singing "Happy Birthday."

A pair of feet entered the den. He could smell a familiar perfume. The steps were quiet as they approached him. Her cool fingers touched his wrist. He waited a moment before opening his eyes.

THE END

About The Author

James Pate is a fiction writer and poet. He was born in Memphis, lived many years in Chicago, and now lives in Shepherdstown, West Virginia.

He is the author of *The Fassbinder Diaries* (Civil Coping Mechanisms), *Flowers Among The Carrion* (Action Books), and *Speed Of Life* (Fahrenheit Press).

He has had work published in Black Warrior Review, Blue Mesa Review, Berkeley Fiction Review, New Delta Review, Cream City Review, Plots with Guns, storySouth, La Petite Zine, Pembroke Magazine, Superstition Review, and Shotgun Honey, among other places.

Acknowledgements

I'd like to thank Scott McFarland, Rajesh Parameswaran, Gene Wildman, Gonzalo Baeza, and Rob Hart, all who, in various ways, helped bring this book into existence.

Thanks to the Virginia Center for the Creative Arts, where the first draft was written one stormy, balmy spring.

Thanks to Johannes Göransson and Joyelle McSweeney, for their extensive knowledge of glam and punk, Big Star and Eggleston, Warhol and the Chelsea Hotel.

Thanks, too, to Fahrenheit Press. The publishing history of this novel is long and bizarre, and Fahrenheit, true to their name, saved it from the ashes.

And I would especially like to thank my wife, Carrie Messenger, for her support and advice, and for patiently reading the multiple drafts of this novel. And for encouraging me to write from my own obsessions, wherever they might lead.

If you enjoyed this book we're sure you'll love these other titles from Fahrenheit Press.

Sparkle Shot by Lina Chern

Jukebox by Saira Viola

All Things Violent by Nikki Dolson

Hidden Depths by Ally Rose

In The Still by Jacqueline Chadwick

Made in the USA
Las Vegas, NV
29 April 2022